OUT OF THE FLAMES

A MYSTERY THRILLER

REBECKA VIGUS

Lilac
Publishing

Book cover, interior book design, and eBook design
by Blue Harvest Creative
www.blueharvestcreative.com

CROSSING THE LINE

Published by
Lilac Publishing

ISBN-13: 978-0989098113
ISBN-10: 0989098117

Visit the author at:
www.ramblingsbyrebecka.blogspot.com
www.facebook.com/RebeckaVigusAuthor
www.twitter.com @DuchessOfLilac

This book is dedicated to
Eric Kline

Follow your dreams

CHAPTER ONE

Certainly the clock showed no more than ten minutes had passed. Already the fire department had arrived. Smoke billowed from the old building into the evening sky. People had gathered to watch and police had cordoned off the area. But he had the perfect view. He could look down on the entire scene. He wondered if everyone had escaped. Soon he would be able to see up close the ravages of the fire.

JAKE WAS STANDING just inside the cordoned area.

For him this was just another routine fire. He knew once the smoke cleared and the fire was out he would be called in to determine how the blaze had started and who might be to blame. He waited patiently out of the way as the smoke billowed and the fire crew did its job. His was a waiting job for now. Later he would sift through the rubble looking for the incendiary device that started it.

Jake overheard the ambulance attendants talking about the people who had been evacuated from the building. Many were senior citizens, others were just getting by. They had lost everything. Most had minor injuries, a couple had been taken to the hospital with smoke inhalation, a child was missing, and there might be a body or two still inside. Jake would know firsthand when the smoke cleared.

The building had been called the Homestead. It was even spelled out in the brick over the entrance. Once it had been a high class hotel. At sometime in the late 1960's the owner had converted it into apartments. They had been luxury apartments for the time. Then the building changed hands and as the neighborhood went down so did the upkeep on the building. Some slum lord owned it now. The apartments were rent controlled, which allowed some low income people to keep them. It was a small building only about eight stories high, but it had gargoyles on the top and some beautiful architecture. It was a shame to see it burn. Jake knew they would never rebuild it.

HE COULDN'T SEE flames anymore, but smoke still rose into the evening sky. It was getting too dark to even see the smoke. Many of the people in the crowd had gone home, to the safety of their apartments and families. He hoped none of them were in buildings which could sell for millions. It made him chuckle. Then he wondered how much the landlord would get from his insurance company, and how much he could hope to gain from this fire.

He walked away from the window. He would go back to it shortly. Now was the time to get things in order. He had a plan and he needed to have everything ready. But the fire pulled him back.

JAKE ROBINS WAS a young man with blonde hair and blue eyes. He had broad shoulders and slender hips. Standing 6'3" there was an air of confidence when he walked. He had played sports in school, but had not really been interested in them. He was more interested in what caused things to happen, although he had not excelled in science either.

Jake spent his time with a couple of buddies playing music. They played Christian music in a church band on some Sundays. Jake found a kind of spiritual peace in the music. He played lead guitar and sometimes sang.

He had a couple of girlfriends along the way, but nothing had been deep or lasting. He wanted an old-fashioned girl. The kind of girl his mom was. He did not care if she had a career, but he was looking for someone solid who could be counted on. Someone who shared his values, and whom he could raise kids with. He figured he would be looking a while longer.

Jake had done two years of criminal justice then joined the police academy. After two years on the police force he got interested in arson investigation. He did a rotation as a fireman and had a lot of respect for the men and women who fought fires for a living. Still he was more interested in why fires started.

Here he was waiting for the chief to give him permission to enter the burned out building and work his magic with the ashes. It was his job to find out how this fire had started.

The coroner had arrived a few minutes ago. It seems there was a body in the basement apartment. Everyone was guessing it was the super. None of the people seemed to know for sure.

"Ain't been a super in that building for years," said one elderly woman. "It's part of the problem; no one wants to fix the things that are broke."

The chief had put in a call to the building owner shortly after he had arrived. So far, Jonathon Billings, III had not arrived on the scene. The news reporters were speculating as to whether or not Billings would show.

When the chief cleared the building, the coroner went in to retrieve the body. He could tell right away fire was not what had killed the man. His skull was bashed in. Once the body had been removed, Jake would enter the building to begin his search for the place where the fire had started

Night had fallen, so for safety reasons, the chief ordered him to keep out and had the area cordoned off. Police officers would remain to make sure no one entered and the third shift would relieve them. Jake would return in the morning to begin his search. He walked down the street to where he had parked his car and headed for home.

CHAPTER TWO

A body had been carried out. A bad omen for sure. Hopefully it would be burned beyond recognition and no one would be on to him. It might be a good time to collect his money and get out of town. He would miss going through the rubble.

He left his perch and went to find a pay phone. It was time to make a call to Mr. Jonathon Billings, III. It was time to collect his due. It was also time to think about leaving Ridge Cliff. His work here was done.

JAKE TOOK A quick shower as soon as he got home. As he headed for the kitchen to find something to eat his phone rang.

"Hello," he said into the mouthpiece.

"Jake, this is Chief McDonald. I'm sorry to bother you at home," the gruff voice came through the phone.

"No problem, Chief," Jake responded. "What's up?"

"The body in the apartment building tonight was an undercover cop."

"Oh, no! Any idea who?" Jake asked anxiously. He still had buddies on the police force.

"Not yet, but his badge was found in his back pocket. Just want you to know this is high priority."

"I'll be there before sun rise, Chief," was Jake's reply.

"Knew I could count on you," said the Chief then he rang off.

Jake just sat there for a minute trying to take it in. He knew the fire was deliberate and it would be up to him to find the evidence. He had better turn in early. He went to the kitchen to find dinner, and then headed to bed.

THE SUN WAS just starting to shine when Jake reached the burned out apartment building. The officers on duty checked his ID then let him go about his business. This was the fourth apartment building which had gone up on the south side of town this month. Somebody was keeping busy. In the others all of the tenants had managed to escape.

Jake wondered what an undercover cop was doing in the basement of the building. Had the fire been set to cover up his murder? It sure seemed likely. Might as well get busy and see what answers he could find.

Jake's kit consisted of a backpack filled with camera, tape recorder, a blue print of the building he had scaled down the night before, drawing pad, latex gloves, surgeon's booties, pens, pencils, glass vials, long tweezers, and a couple of small clean paint cans. He was ready to collect the evidence as soon as he put on his booties and gloves. He readied his camera and started toward the basement.

One of the officers stopped him saying, "It will be easier to get to the basement if you use the alley entrance. Go down the right side of the building and enter at the back."

"Thanks," Jake said over his shoulder as he headed toward the right side of the building to follow the man's instructions.

Jake put on headphones and cranked up his Ipod. His was a lonely job so; he listened to music as he collected evidence. Today it would be his favorite group Thousand Foot Krutch. Once he found the entrance he stopped and put on the gloves and booties. He got out his camera and a small tape recorder so he could record what he saw. It would save him time later when he was putting together his report. Carefully he went into the basement.

It was easy to see why no one had been able to get out of here. There were the remnants of boxes and crates everywhere. Jake adjusted the camera and took photos so he could remember the scene as he first saw it. Then slowly he moved through looking for the origin of the fire and any incendiary fluids or devices. It was going to be a long morning.

HE HAD A hard time getting through to Billings last night. The servant on the line told him Billings was not taking any calls. It took about fifteen minutes to convince the idiot this was not the press and it was an emergency. He remembered Billings nasally voice as he came on the line.

"Jonathon Billings, here."

"Of course you're there. It's where I'd expected you to be," he replied.

"Who is this? What kind of prank is this?" Billings demanded.

"No, prank, Billings. This is the man you owe for getting the Homestead torn down."

"What are you talking about?" Billings asked anxiously.

"The Homestead, you remember the building?"

"Of course, I know the building, I own it!" he shouted.

"Well, you do, however; the fire department is going to be interested in why it burned. You don't want them to know about it now do you?"

"What do you mean burned?" Billings screamed. Then, "Wait a minute." Billings placed his hand over the mouthpiece to listen to his butler.

"Mr. Jonathon, the fire department called a couple of hours ago to say one of your apartment buildings was on fire. You were in a meeting and didn't want to be disturbed so I just took the message."

"Oh, good Lord, man!" Billings exclaimed. Into the phone he said, "I don't know what paper you are with, but I have no comment at this time.

"I'm not with any paper or news team. I'm the man who set fire to your building."

"What!!!" Billings shrieked.

"You heard me. Now calm down, Billings and I'll tell you how this is all going to work," said the man on the phone.

"I demand to know what you are talking about!"

"I'm talking about the payment you are going to make to me so I don't tell the cops you hired me to burn your building.

"I did no such thing," Billings protested.

"Of course you did. Here is how it works. If you pay me the amount I ask for, I don't take a tape recording of you hiring me to the press."

"What tape recording?" Billings asked suspiciously.

He went on to tell Billings about the recording made in Billings' office, where to send the bearer bonds, how many to send, and in what denominations. Billings had sputtered and protested, but after hearing some of the recording was able to see the advantages of paying up. He was also very specific about when the money was due.

Oh, yes, it was going to be worth it now. He would be leaving the cold and with this fire pay off could retire in style south of this country's borders.

He was not going to spend any more time in this town than necessary. He had no desire to get caught. He had just come from the post office where he filed a change of address. The cops would never catch him now.

CHAPTER THREE

J ake spent the better part of the morning taking pictures and making a voice recording of what he saw. Most of the damage had been from smoke and water. He had been able to climb the stairs and look into most of the apartments. He was relieved to know the people who lived here would be able to salvage something not a common occurrence in most fires. Although he doubted the building would be rebuilt.

He was going back through the basement on his way out when something caught his eye. He readied his camera and walked slowly toward it. He wondered how he had missed something shiny in all the charred ruins.

In the floor was what appeared to be a door. The handle must have been covered when he went through earlier. He photographed the handle then slowly started to lift it. There was too much debris covering it. He sat his pack and camera down and started to uncover the door. Once uncovered, he photographed it again. Before entering, he called for the officers on duty.

Bob Benson the first to arrive asked, "What did you find?"

"It appears to be some kind of door," Jake replied. "I'm going to open it, but I wanted you to know so if there is any evidence you'll know where it came from."

"Sounds good," said Benson as he came forward.

Together the two men lifted the door. There appeared to be steps going down. Jake pulled out a flash light. He slowly moved the light around the opening.

"I can see a chamber or something off the right," he said. "I'm going down for a better look."

"Okay, I'll stay here."

The second officer, Matt Walsh arrived just as Jake was descending the stairs. "What's going on?"

"We found some kind of passage or storage place," Benson responded. "Fire guy is going down."

Both men stood at the top as Jake made his way down the stairs. His light flickered a couple of times. He stepped off the bottom and to the right.

"There are a bunch of things stored down here," he called up. "Some of it is water damaged, but most is dry. You'll want to have someone come and haul it up. We need to see what it is. What the...."

"What is it?" the men asked in unison.

"There are several tunnels down here." Then, "It's okay, I won't hurt you. Come on, we'll find your family."

The men looked at each other as if Jake had lost his mind.

"Fellas, I found the missing child. You want to send for an ambulance?"

"Well, I'll be."

"This is unit seven at the Homestead, roll a bus, we have a survivor."

"Wait until the news gets a hold of this," Walsh said.

"No!" Jake said surprising them both. "This child might be a witness."

"You're right," Benson replied. "I hadn't thought of that."

The tousled dark head of the child was buried in Jake's shoulder as he came up the stairs. He could hear the ambulance in the distance. He smiled down at the child in his arms, "See I told you it would be okay."

Luminous brown eyes just looked up at him. Under the dirt and grime this child was beautiful.

The ambulance attendants quickly took the child's vitals and put a temporary splint on the leg. As they started to load the child into the ambulance Jake stood up. The child quickly grabbed his arm.

"It's okay, little one," Jake said softly. "They will take good care of you."

The child's head swung from side to side and tears began to roll down the child's grimy cheeks.

"Why don't you ride along?" one of the attendants suggested.

"Okay, give me a minute to grab my pack," Jake responded. To the child he said, "I'll be right back."

Jake quickly grabbed his backpack and camera then walked to the ambulance. He said to Benson, "Keep an eye on my car. I'll be back to get it later."

Benson nodded and Jake boarded the ambulance for the ride to the hospital.

THE RIDE TO the hospital was uneventful. The child clung to Jake's hand while the paramedics hung an IV and made small talk. At the hospital Jake walked in with the gurney but had to stay outside the exam room. The child became frantic so the nurses finally let Jake in.

"Are you family," asked the nurse.

"Nope, I just found him in the basement of a burned out building," Jake replied.

"Well, you are going to be in for a surprise. Your he, is a she," chuckled the nurse.

Jake looked from the child to the nurse but said nothing.

"Any idea her name or where she came from?"

"Nope. I was checking to see what caused the fire at the Homestead last night and found a door under the basement. When I went to look, I found her huddled in a corner whimpering."

"We'll get social services in here to see if they know her," the nurse replied.

"When will she be in a room?" Jake asked.

17

"She probably won't be. They will set her leg and turn her over to social services. They'll put her in foster care."

Jake was not pleased with the idea. The girl could be a witness to what happened at the Homestead. The cop in him said she needed protection. He looked at the little girl who clung to his hand.

"I have to make a phone call. I will be right back," he said gently.

She turned her luminous eyes on him and nodded.

Jake quickly walked outside and dialed a number on his cell phone.

"McDonald, here," the chief said when he answered.

"Chief, we have a problem. I found a child in the sub-basement of the Homestead. She has a broken leg and is in Mercy Hospital. They want to turn her over to social services. I think she could be a witness and needs protection until we can find out who she is and what she saw," Jake said quickly into his phone.

"Where are you?" the chief asked.

"Mercy Hospital, with the girl. I have all the samples in my kit."

"Stay there; I'll see what I can do. Can you stay with her until I can make arrangements?'

"Sure, what about the samples for the lab?"

"Just hold them. I should be there in half an hour."

"Okay."

Jake closed the phone and walked back in to see what he could learn about his new charge.

The nurses were hovering around the little girl whose eyes lit up when she saw Jake.

"You sure are her hero," one nurse remarked.

Jake blushed and said, "So it would seem."

The child reached for his hand as he neared the bed and the nurses left them alone.

"Well, sweetheart," Jake began, "can you tell me your name?"

"Lupe," she replied with a smile.

"And how old are you Miss Lupe?" Jake asked.

"Six."

"What is your last name?"

"Sullivan."

"Do you know where your mom and dad are? I should call them."

"I don't have a mom and dad," the child said sadly.

"You must live with someone," Jake said softly.

"Papa and Nana," the child said her eyes brightening.

"Good," Jake said with a smile. "I'm going to check with the nurses and see if we can find them."

Lupe squeezed his hand and said, "Please don't go."

"I'll just be right outside," he answered.

"Please, don't go. The bad man will come."

"Who is the bad man, Lupe?" Jake asked.

"The man in the basement who hurt Mr. Mike," she replied.

"Did you see what happened to Mr. Mike?" Jake asked.

"Yes, before I went into the tunnels."

"Can you tell me what happened, Lupe?" he asked gently.

Lupe only shook her head and squeezed his hand.

"Okay, Lupe, I will stay," Jake said. "My boss is coming soon. Is it alright if I ask a nurse to come in so we can find your Papa and Nana?"

Lupe nodded her curly head. Jake pushed the call button and waited for a nurse to arrive.

CHAPTER FOUR

Meanwhile across town a man waited in the shadow of a doorway to see if anyone entered the mailbox drop. He had rented the box months ago and it had served its purpose well. Three other executives had made substantial money drops to it or one like it.

The sun was high and traffic was steady; as the man waited he pretended to read the newspaper. So far no one had gone near his box today. He hoped he would not have to make another call to Jonathon Billings III. If he did it would only add to the amount of his current request. It would also delay his departure plans. He was becoming impatient, when he noticed a man looking very furtive as he approached the mailbox. This could be it. As he watched a few minutes more, he began to smile. Billings had come through and he would soon be on his way.

JAKE ASKED THE nurse if she would check and see if either of the Sullivans had been admitted to the hospital. She said she would check and let him know. She was back quickly and asked if she could talk to him in private.

"Lupe, I need to talk to the nurse. I will be right outside and I will not let the bad man in. Okay?" Jake said softly to the child.

Lupe nodded and let go of his hand. Her eyes never left him as he stepped outside the curtain.

The nurse, whose name was Susan, said quietly, "There were two Sullivans admitted after the fire. Both of them are elderly. Mrs. Sullivan died of smoke inhalation and Mr. Sullivan has not spoken since."

"Is there any way Mr. Sullivan could be brought down here?" Jake asked.

"I'll see what I can do," she replied. "Do you think he is Lupe's grandfather?"

"He might be. And if he thinks he's lost everything he will give up."

"I'll let you know," she said.

"Thank you." As she walked away, Jake went back to sit at Lupe's bedside.

"Did they find my Nana and Papa?" she asked expectantly.

"I'm not sure, they are still checking," Jake replied. He hoped the man upstairs was her grandfather and she would be his reason to live. Otherwise he didn't know what would happen to Lupe.

CHIEF MCDONALD SHOWED up just as Mr. Sullivan was wheeled into the room.

"Papa!" shouted Lupe.

Mr. Sullivan looked up and a smile creased his wrinkled face. "Lupe," he said wondrously. "I thought we lost you in the fire."

"No, Papa, I was in the tunnels," Lupe explained. "I was hiding from the bad man."

Mr. Sullivan looked from the chief to Jake and back at Lupe. "What bad man is she talking about?"

"We don't know yet," Jake answered. "Lupe, has not..."

"Jake saved me," she interrupted. "He found me in the tunnels and brought me here in the ambulance."

"Lupe," her grandfather began, "you are not supposed to interrupt."

"I'm sorry, Papa, and Jake," she said with her head hanging down.

"It's alright, little one," Jake said ruffling her hair with his fingers.

She quickly brightened and asked her grandfather, "When can we go home, Papa? Where is Nana?"

Mr. Sullivan shook his head sadly then said, "Lupe, Nana has gone to be with the angels and I'm not sure we have a home."

Lupe began to cry. Jake lifted her onto her grandfather's lap and he comforted the little girl. Then Jake and Chief McDonald left the room.

"What's going to happen to them, Chief?" Jake asked.

"I've got a place they can stay no one knows about. You and I will take them there as soon as they are discharged. I've arranged with Captain Holloway for two plain clothes guys to meet us here and follow us. They will remain on duty and be relieved at the end of their shift with two more until we know what the little girl knows and can find them a permanent safe place."

"Thanks, Chief," Jake said.

"I'm glad you found her."

"Me, too. No telling how long she would have been down there with a broken leg."

Once the hospital released Mr. Sullivan and Lupe, Jake and the Chief took them to his hunting lodge out of town. Two plain clothes officers followed behind. Once situated in their new home, Jake went to stock up on some groceries. He told them he would make lunch and check in with them every day, but he had to get to work to find out who set the fire.

AFTER A TIME, he felt it was safe. So, he went back to his dumpy rented room and waited. He knew the drop had been made. It would be tomorrow before it was sent to the new mailbox. He looked over some travel brochures he had picked up. He was thinking the Mexican Riviera looked inviting or maybe Rio de Janeiro.

He flopped on the bed, turned on the TV, and channel surfed until he nodded off to sleep. He dreamed of warm tropical climates and lazy days on the beach. Hunger was what woke him.

He trudged down the stairs and out into the evening in search of food. He couldn't risk going by the Homestead as much as he wanted to.

CHAPTER FIVE

Jake went straight to the lab after having lunch with the Sullivans. He sent his pictures to the photo lab and began taking out his samples so he could begin tests.

Then he began the slow process of logging each item he had taken from the scene. Each might hold the clue to what started the fire.

The phone behind him rang, "Robins, here."

"Chief McDonald. They have the name of the officer killed in the fire. You need to come to my office there is going to be a briefing on what we know so far."

"I can be there in just a few minutes," Jake replied.

"See you then." The chief disconnected.

Jake set aside his work and headed for the Chief's office. He wondered who the dead officer was and if what the Chief had learned would help or hinder his case.

Jake knocked when he reached the Chief's office.

"Enter." He entered slowly and found the room filled with people.

"Good you're here. We'll begin with introductions," the Chief said. "This is Jake Robins, my arson investigator. Jake, this is Lt. Martin Watson, homicide and Detective Rachel Adams. This is Dr. Mark Clark, from the medical examiner's office and this is Ramon Martinez from the District Attorney's office." Jake shook hands all around then took the last seat in the room.

The Chief began by turning the conversation over to Lt. Watson. Watson was a big man. He stood well over six feet and had the skin tone of dark chocolate. He would be an imposing presence if met in a dark alley.

"According to the badge found in the deceased's pocket, he was Detective Mike Desmond, assigned to our undercover unit," Watson said. "Dr. Clark would you give us all the preliminary autopsy report?"

Dr. Clark was an unimposing person. His features were so ordinary he would be missed in a crowd. He handed everyone a sheet of paper then said, "So, you are all on the same page, we found Officer Desmond was killed by a blunt force trauma to the back of his head. He was then burned beyond recognition."

"How was he identified?" asked Detective Adams.

"We were able to get dental records."

"Thank you."

Lt. Watson then said, "Detective Adams, were you able to find out what Officer Desmond was working on?"

"Yes," she said firmly as she stood to address those in the room. She was surprisingly tall for a woman, approximately five feet ten inches. Her auburn hair was pulled severely back and in a bun at the nape of her neck. "He had been assigned as an undercover agent to see if he could determine why the buildings in the area were being torched."

"Had he made any headway? What exactly was his cover?" asked the Lieutenant.

"I've not seen his case notes yet or talked to his contact in the department, so I'm not sure what he'd found. He went under after the first fire. His cover had him as a homeless vagrant."

"Do you have any idea why he might have been in the basement of the Homestead last night?"

"It appears the residents had allowed him to stay in the old super's apartment in the basement because he was doing some simple handyman chores for them."

"Thank you. Any questions so far?" Seeing none he moved on. "I understand Mr. Robins has found us a witness."

Jake startled to hear his name responded, "Yes, sir. A young child who lived in the building was found early this morning in the tunnels under the building. She has said something about a bad man, but so far it's all we can get from her."

"Thank you. This is one thing we do NOT want the media to know. She and her guardian have been put in a secure place with police protection until we can get more information and can ensure their safety."

"Robins, do you have any cause of the blaze yet?"

"Not yet, sir. I do know Officer Desmond was the point of origin for the blaze," he hesitated then said, "I also know there was something going on in the building. I don't know whether or not the residents knew about it though."

"Would you like to elaborate?"

"In the tunnels under the Homestead there are several crates. Some of the crates had been moved to the basement area and were destroyed. I did not open the crates once I found the child."

"Detective Adams, you and Robins will be a team. Both of you will be present when the crates are opened. I'd like to see them opened yet today."

"Yes, Sir," they said in unison.

"Is there anything you would like to add, Mr. Martinez?"

"Not at this time, I am here as liaison with the district attorney's office." He was a small man who looked very out of place in his grey suit and starched white shirt. Jake thought he would have looked more at home in a street gang.

"Thank you. Is there anything else to add?" He looked at each person then said, "You all have a job to do. We will be back here at 9:00 a.m. sharp, hopefully with some answers, dismissed."

Each rose and left the room. On the way out Detective Adams caught up with Jake and asked, "Is there some time we could meet and talk? We need to be on the same page if we are to work together."

Jake responded, "I need an hour to get some tests started then I should be able to meet you at the Homestead. We can check out the boxes in the tunnels."

"See you then."

BACK IN HIS flea bag room, he paced. It would take another day for the mail to reach his new post office box. Then he would be on the next plane out of here. His first stop would be Rio de Janeiro. He could hardly wait. He had seen the last cold winter of his life. He was bored waiting. He looked out the window at the Homestead. They still had cops on duty there. Odd usually they left once the arson guys were done. He wondered if it had to do with the body. He so wanted to see what his art had done.

Restless he paced for a while then went back to channel surfing on the TV. Waiting was one thing he hated. There was a big risk in getting caught if you had to wait too long. He was already later than he had planned to be, this last fire had been a fluke. He had enough from the first fires to live comfortably the rest of his life, but he could not resist just one more fire.

IT WAS ALMOST three o'clock by the time Jake got back to the Homestead. Detective Adams was waiting for him there.

"Sorry to keep you waiting," he said.

"No, problem. Here's my card with my cell phone, home and office numbers on it," she said handing him the card. "Next time call."

Jake blushed as he took the card. He reached for his pocket notebook and jotted his phone numbers for his cell, the lab and his home and handed them to her. She nodded.

"So, where are these crates?"

"This way," he said leading her to the back of the building. He waved to Officers Benson and Walsh. They waved back.

Once inside both took out their flashlights, the door to the tunnels remained open.

"It's this way," Jake said as he started down the stairs. He pulled out his camera so he could photograph whatever they found.

It didn't take them long to find the first passageway. Jake led the way. Once there he set his flashlight on one of the crates. He was holding his camera and a crowbar.

"Would you like to open it or shall I?" he asked.

"I'll open it and you can take your pictures," she responded reaching for the crow bar.

Jake handed her the crow bar and got his camera ready. Detective Adams had also set her flashlight on a crate to give them as much light as possible. Carefully Adams wedged the crow bar between the slats and opened the crate.

Both of them let out a big breath when the crate did not explode. Jake helped to move the top and Detective Adams removed some of the packing so they could see what was in there.

"Oh, my God!" she exclaimed. "It's a wonder this place didn't take the whole block down."

Jake said nothing and began taking pictures. Inside the box were several different types of guns. There were sniper rifles, AK 47's, M16's, Mac 10's, and assorted handguns. When he was done with the pictures he said, "There must not be any ammo down here."

"We'll have to look in each box. I'm going up top to radio for a wagon to take these in."

"I'm sure glad these are not on the street," Jake said.

"Me, too."

Jake remained in the basement and pried open another crate. This one had shoulder missile launchers in it. He took photos from all angles and touched nothing. To his mind, someone was going to start a war somewhere and he was glad they could stop it.

CHAPTER SIX

Two hours after the find, Jake was back in his lab. His pictures from earlier in the day had arrived. He looked at those as he ran some tests. He still wasn't sure what accelerant was used. He had narrowed down the incendiary device to either a match book or cigarettes. A couple more tests would tell him which one. A knock on the door caught him looking at the photos.

"Hi, hope you don't mind my dropping in?" Detective Adams said.

"Nope. Just about finished for today. Was there something you needed?"

"I was hoping we could grab some dinner and spend some time going over Desmond's notes," she said expectantly.

"Sure. Do you want take out?" he asked.

"Doesn't matter."

"I know a great Italian take-out just down the block from my apartment. We can eat and go through the notes there."

"Okay, when do you want to meet?"

Jake put away the photos, turned, and said, "I'm ready now."

She had changed into jeans and a dark brown sweater. Her auburn hair was down and the transformation took his breath away. He had known she was tall, but her willowy shape had escaped him in her uniform. She smiled and said, "Okay, then."

Armed with warm garlic bread, lasagna, and a panna cotta with fresh strawberries for dessert, Rachel and Jake climbed the three flights to Jake's apartment. As Rachel put the food on the table Jake found dishes and silverware.

"Would you like, wine, beer, coffee, Coke, or water to drink?" he asked.

"Wine would be nice, but I'll stick with coffee. I want a clear head to go through these case notes."

"Coffee it is." Jake grabbed two cups and started the coffee maker. They had a pleasant meal. Jake learned Rachel was the second of three girls. She was the tomboy of the three so police work was a good choice for her. Jake told her he had five half-siblings who were scattered to the four winds. They talked about their jobs and when dinner was over Jake loaded the dishwasher.

They moved to the living room to start going through Desmond's case notes.

"Did you know Desmond?" Jake asked.

"I met him once. Did you know him?"

"I never met him. I was wondering if he had any family."

"He was born in Jamaica. I guess his parents still live there. His file doesn't say. It doesn't mention any next of kin. His birth name was Miguel," she replied reading the file.

"He was the perfect undercover cop."

"How so?"

"He has no immediate family to will worry about him. No next of kin to report him missing. The only person who would know if something was wrong would be his partner."

"I see what you mean," she said. Stretching she said, "I need to go home. Let's get this cleaned up."

"Can you leave it with me?"

"Sure, if you want."

Jake walked Rachel down to her car and watched her drive away. Then he returned to his apartment. Turned on the late news and picked up the file.

IN A SHABBY room across town someone else was watching the news when the newscaster said, "This just in... the Ridge Cliff Police Department confiscated a cache of weapons from tunnels under the Homestead. If you recall, the Homestead burned earlier this week and an undercover police officer was killed. We'll keep you informed as we get more information."

"Well I'll be. Someone is going to be pretty angry about," he said to himself. It also explained why cops were still on duty. He knew his money had better be in the mailbox in the morning or there was going to be trouble. He wanted out of this town. And he wanted out NOW.

He shut off the TV and tried to get some sleep. He knew it would be fruitless, though as he punched his fist into his pillow.

THE NEXT MORNING found Jake doing a gas spectrometer test and doing burn tests on different fabrics to see how long the clothing on Officer Desmond had burned before igniting the building. He also had some other samples he had collected which were undergoing tests.

He reached for the envelope holding the photos he had taken of the scene. It was time to put them on his board and listen to what he recorded at the time. He needed to get a feel for what he had seen.

There were pictures of where the body had been. He could see the white tape where the body had been found. He could see where the burn pattern had been and how the empty crates in the basement had been good tinder for the fire. He could see the places which were dark like maybe there had been liquid of some type on them. Then he saw what he was looking for. There in the seventh picture was the burn line. The spot where the arsonist stood to start his fire. He could see how the fire had led straight to the body of Officer Desmond.

He hung the pictures on his bulletin board and went back to his work table. There it was the pack of matches which had set the whole thing in motion. It looked like a cigarette had been lit and placed in the matchbook. Allowing it to burn down and set the book of matches on fire. The matches then ignited the gas poured on the body and led away to make the line on the floor. Someone stood there quite a while to make sure the fire started. Someone who had a working knowledge of fires.

Jake wanted to see the notes and write ups on the other fires. He would make comparisons and see if they could come up with a profile of the arsonist.

For now he was going to check in on the Sullivans then make a call to Detective Adams and see if she had found anything new for them to work with. He picked up the phone and called Detective Adams at her office. She was not at her desk. He left a message and tried her cell phone.

"Adams."

"Jake Robins here. Is there some time we can meet today?"

"Sure. Do you need me right away?"

"Not really. I was going to go have lunch with the Sullivans. I thought you might want to meet them."

"Give me half an hour and I'll be at your office to pick you up."

"Okay." Jake hung up his phone and then quickly picked it up and dialed the Chief.

"McDonald."

"Chief, this is Jake Robins."

"What can I do for you?" ask the Chief.

"I need to see the notes and tests on the other fires. I need to see if there are any parallels."

"I'll make a call and have them sent to you today."

"Okay, I'm leaving in about half an hour to go out to check on the Sullivans. I'm taking Detective Adams with me.

"Good thinking. Keep me posted."

They rang off. Jake called the Sullivans to tell them he was bringing Rachel with him and then, went back to his pictures and tests.

CHAPTER SEVEN

He had been cooped up as long as he could stand it. He knew how police procedure worked. They would spend time going through the files on the other fires. They would run more tests. He had to get out of town.

He locked the door to his room and headed down the stairs. He was not getting into the rickety elevator. Besides he had a fear of small spaces. At ground level he looked both ways before heading south.

He looked again at the light then crossed the street and went into the park. He wandered through the park as though it were just a morning walk for him. On the other side he looked both ways and behind him. He did not spot a tail, so he turned right and crossed another street then entered a little greasy spoon diner called Sal's. He took a seat at the counter.

A tired looking waitress brought him coffee and said, "What can I get you?"

He answered, "I'll have two eggs scrambled, sausage, and a short stack."

"Be back shortly."

He nodded and picked up a newspaper lying on the counter. There was nothing on the front page about the progress in finding the arsonist. There was no mention of the dead cop either, so he turned to the stock pages to see how the Dow closed.

The waitress was back in a few minutes with his order.

"Do you need anything else?"

"Just some more coffee, please."

"Sure thing." She went to get the coffee pot and poured some more for him.

A few minutes later a couple of beat cops came in. They took a booth.

"Millie, a black and a black and tan," one of them called to the waitress.

"Be right there boys," she answered.

She took them their coffees and asked if they were having the usual.

Both said yes then one of them asked, "How's Benny doing these days?"

"He's working at a garage and stayin' out of trouble," she said, then added, "for now any way."

"Good news," was the reply.

She went back and gave the order to the cook. He finished his meal and left the money on the counter along with a tip, then left and walked back toward the park. Neither cop had even noticed him.

After crossing the park he headed toward his mailbox. Once there he looked around to make sure he did not have a tail then he went in to retrieve his package.

He walked quickly back to his hotel room to count his money. He counted it twice. This couldn't be. It was short. The money had not all been paid. What kind of trick was Billings playing? He put the money in a battered suitcase and put the suitcase in the closet. He then went downstairs to find a pay phone.

He dialed the number for Billings's office. The secretary answered, "Mr. Billings's office, how may I help you?"

"Jonathon Billings please."

"May I tell him whose calling?"

"Yes, tell him it's the police, regarding the fire at the Homestead."

"Yes, sir, I'll put you right through."

"Jonathon Billings, how can I be of service?" he said in his most charming voice.

"What kind of trick are you trying to pull? Where is my money?"

"I sent it."

"Not all of it you didn't. I want the rest now!"

"How do you propose we do that?"

"Get to your bank, pick up the money and go to the city park. Enter on the west side of the park. Walk to the center and then head east. There is a thick stand of brush on the south side, when no one is looking, place your briefcase in the brush and walk on. Your driver can pick you up on the east side of the park. Don't pull anything funny. No cops or you will be news at six and eleven."

"I cannot walk out in the middle of a business day."

"You can and you will or I will take the tape to the nearest TV station and you will find yourself having dinner in the jail. If you are not there within the hour that is exactly what will happen."

"I see," said Billings. "Let me arrange to take an early lunch and I will follow your directions."

"To the letter, no screw ups."

"I understand. Thank you for calling."

"The clock is ticking, Billings."

He hung up the phone and hailed a taxi. He planned to follow Billings to see there was no screw up.

DETECTIVE ADAMS WAS true to her word and thirty minutes later she strolled into Jake's lab.

"Ready to roll, Robins?" she asked.

Jake nodded his head. He looked up from the microscope he had been peering into. "Take a look at this will you?"

Adams came toward him and looked into the scope. "What am I seeing?" she asked.

"Hair follicles."

"Whose?"

"Not our victim. I have the labs and notes from the other fires coming over this afternoon. Maybe there will be a match in those."

"You mean this could be from our pyro?"

"Yep," he said. "Now let's go meet the Sullivans."

They walked out to the parking lot and took the car assigned to Detective Adams. Jake gave directions. He explained he had called ahead to let them know they were coming.

"Lupe was thrilled. She's never met a woman police officer before," Jake said chuckling.

"I hope she won't be disappointed."

"She won't be."

Rachel gave him a sidelong look.

"What?" he asked.

"Just wondering about your last comment."

"Take it as a compliment."

She nodded and they drove the rest of the way in silence.

Lupe was waiting for them at the door when they arrived. She threw herself at Jake.

"She's pretty."

"Yep, she is," Jake agreed.

Rachel blushed and asked if there was anything she could do to help with lunch.

"Nope," Lupe said with a grin. "Papa and me fixed something special and I set the table by myself."

"Well, then lead the way," Jake said as he put her down.

Lupe in a boot cast awkwardly scampered ahead of them into the kitchen/dining area. The table was set for four and there were flowers in a vase. Mr. Sullivan was in the kitchen.

"Have a seat, I'll be right there."

The three of them sat and Mr. Sullivan brought lunch to the table.

Rachel was surprised to see he had made tossed salad, beef stew and dumplings.

"What a feast!" she exclaimed. "I wasn't expecting this."

"I thought you would be expecting sandwiches and Lupe and I wanted you to know how grateful we are for you putting us up," Mr. Sullivan said. Then he turned to Lupe, "Will you say grace for us?"

Lupe nodded and bowed her head. "Thank you Lord for the food we are about to eat and for Jake saving me and finding Papa. Thank you for having him bring his friend to have lunch with us, and take good care of Nana. Amen."

"Amen," came the sound of the other three voices.

Mr. Sullivan asked Rachel if she would be kind enough to serve every one. She did.

They made small talk as they ate. Lupe kept everyone from thinking about what brought them all together. After lunch Jake and Rachel did the dishes and put them away. Finally they walked into the living room.

"Lupe, can I ask you some questions?" Rachel asked.

"Sure, what do you want to know?"

"Well, can you tell me how you got into the tunnels the last time you went in?"

"I was with Mr. Mike in the basement and he heard someone trying to get in. So, he told me to go to the tunnels and go out the secret door, but the door was stuck."

"Do you know what happened to Mr. Mike?"

"Yes, the bad man came. He and Mr. Mike were yelling. Then the bad man hit Mr. Mike when he turned to go away."

"Do you know what he hit him with?"

"It looked like a bat."

"What did you do then?"

"I dropped the secret door and ran. When I couldn't get out the secret door I tried to go back to the basement, but I fell and broke my leg."

"You were very brave," Rachel said. "One more thing, Lupe, do you know the bad man's name?"

"No."

"Lupe, I'm going to send someone out here. Will you tell him what the bad man looks like? He can draw a picture on his computer if you tell him."

"I think so."

"Good, girl." Rachel turned to Mr. Sullivan. "Thank you again for lunch."

"It was my pleasure," he turned to Jake and said, "You be sure to bring her back again."

Jake smiled and said, "I will." He tousled Lupe's hair as they went out the door.

"She's quite a kid," Rachel said as they headed back to the city and work.

"Yep, she is," Jake said absently.

"What are you thinking, Robins?"

"Will you swing by the Homestead?"

"Sure, did you think of something?"

"Lupe said there was a secret door. I'd like to look in the sub-basement again."

"Sounds good to me

CHAPTER EIGHT

It had been almost an hour. He was already in place. Billings should be here any minute. He had taken all sorts of precautions. He had walked the perimeter of the park three times. There was no sign of cops. So far Billings was following the rules. He glanced at his watch and then at the west entrance to the park.

Jonathon Billings III was not a man used to taking orders, however he thought this time he should probably make an exception. It galled him some flunky criminal could have been at his meeting and recorded his off-hand comments. He had security in his office three times today looking for bugs. They hadn't found any. Now here he was walking into the park in the middle of the afternoon with a briefcase full of money. Money he was just supposed to toss in the bushes. He was angry.

He chuckled as Billings stomped through the park. The man had no idea how to appreciate the things around him. Well, it was his own fault. If he had followed the first directions he would not be here. Neither one of them would be.

Billings did as he was told and tossed the briefcase into the bushes. He also looked around to see if anyone had noticed or was heading toward him. He wanted a look at this scumbag. There was no one in sight. Billings shrugged and moved to the east exit and his warm car. He looked back again as he was about to get in, but still saw no one. At least he saw no one in the bushes the park seemed to have few people in it and those who were there were quickly heading to other places.

Once Billings had driven away he waited another ten minutes to be sure Billings did not have a tail. Then he headed down to the bushes by a different route than Billings had taken. He slipped in and transferred the money to a battered briefcase he had hidden there earlier. He wanted to be sure there was no tracking device in the briefcase Billings had left. He took a quick check, saw no one in the area and headed to the west entrance to the park. He had his money and he was going to make arrangements to leave town today.

JAKE AND RACHEL waved to the cops on duty and headed for the basement. Rachel was carrying a flashlight. They went to the now empty sub-basement and began to search.

"I think the door must be near where I found Lupe," Jake said.

"Okay, lead the way," said Rachel handing him the flashlight.

Jake led the way into the chamber where he had found Lupe. "I don't see any stairs, but she said she fell."

"Wait. Look over to the left."

"I see it."

They walked the direction Rachel had indicated. There were several blocks piled up to look like stairs. Together they walked up them.

"It looks like an old door. The knob is gone."

"I'll push and see what happens," said Jake.

The door did not budge.

"Someone must have put something against it."

"Do you want to go outside and look or do you want to stay here?"

"I'll stay if you can find your way out with out the light."

"Brave, girl," he said chuckling. She laughed too as he headed back the way he had come.

It took about ten minutes for Jake to find the spot on the outside of the building. There had been an old shed attached to the building. The fire had taken it down and dropped the roof in front of the door. It took him another ten minutes to clear debris out of the way so he could open the door.

"Looks like we found the secret door."

"Yep, and I know why she couldn't get out," Jake said. "Do you think we can have dinner again tonight? I have some things I need to bounce off you."

"Sure. I'll come by around seven."

They headed back to the car. Rachel dropped Jake back at the lab and went on to the squad room.

In the lab, Jake found the tests, notes, and samples taken from the previous fires. He sat down and began reading through the notes. He had just about finished the first one when the phone rang.

"Robins."

"Jake, it's Rachel. We've got a problem."

"What kind of problem?"

"Not on the phone. Gather everything you've got and I'll be there in half an hour. We're taking everything with us."

"Rather melodramatic isn't it?"

"Not when you hear what I have. See you soon."

Rachel hung up the phone and Jake got busy putting all the notes, tests, and samples in a box. Then he gathered up the notes, test results, and sample he had run. He could not imagine why Rachel thought they had to play cloak and dagger, but he would go along for now. He was ready when she arrived. She picked up one box and he grabbed the other. They said nothing all the way out of the building.

He saw they were taking Rachel's personal car, a sleek black Chevy Malibu with a moon roof.

Once in the car he asked, "Okay, what gives?"

She nodded her head no and drove on out of the city. Once they were out of the city in a wooded area she pulled off the road, stopped the car, and got out with a small box in her hand. She walked slowly around the car then shouted, "Bingo!" She reached under the rim of the back passenger tire and pulled something out. She tossed it as far as she could into the woods. Then she motioned for Jake to get out of the car. She pulled a different item out of her jacket and started going over the seats in the car. Under the passenger seat she reached down and pulled something out. Again she threw it as far as she could into the woods.

"Okay, we can get back in."

They got into the car and Jake said, "You need to tell me what is going on."

"We got an ID on the 'bad man' from Lupe."

"I'd say it's a good thing."

"Normally I would agree; however 'bad man' is a former cop, who liaisoned with the fire department."

"Great!"

"Not great. No one has seen him for about eight months. There was some kind of trouble over a drug bust. I don't know all the details. He left in disgrace and vowed he would get even. Jake, my car was bugged and had a tracer on it. I don't know who might still be working with him."

"Oh, man! What do we do now?"

"Well, first we are going to have to relocate the Sullivans tonight. Then we are going to have to find some place for us to stay. Is there anyone you trust in the fire department we can stay in touch with?"

"I've always trusted Chief McDonald. He's a straight up guy."

"Okay, we'll get one of those throw away phones and call him."

They drove to the local discount store went in and bought a pre-paid phone and a thousand minutes. They asked in the store if they could get it programmed there. The clerk walked them through the steps and had their minutes added. They thanked him and left.

Back in the car, Jake called Chief McDonald.

"McDonald here."

"Chief, this is Jake. We have a situation here. Will you take your cell phone and leave the building, then call me back at this number?"

"Sounds a bit cloak and dagger, Robins."

"I know, Chief, but this is life threatening."

"Give me five minutes."

"Thanks, Chief," Jake said then he hung up the phone. "He said he needs five minutes."

"Okay."

They waited what seemed an eternity then the phone rang.

"Robins."

"What's going on, Jake, and it better be good," the Chief demanded.

"We have identified a possible suspect and he's a former police officer. Adams' car was bugged and had a tracking device on it."

"Okay, what do you need from me?"

"We're going to pick up the Sullivans and find a new safe house. Adams and I will work from there. This will be the only number you can reach us on and we need you to keep us in the loop as well as keep everyone away from us."

"I can make it happen. Jake, take whatever you need from the cabin. I'll handle things here. Do you have a new location in mind?" He paused then asked, "Who is this former officer anyway?"

"I'm not sure yet where we will go, but I'm working on it. Our possible suspect is a cop named Mark Stone. The only other person who knows is the sketch artist and he is still with the Sullivans. "

"Mark Stone!!! He's the creep who used to be attached to the fire department."

"He's the one, Chief," Jake said. "One more thing, can you tell me if there is a back way out of your hunting cabin?"

"Yeah, there is a two track out behind the place. Take it for a mile and veer right at the fork. It will take you to the main road. You'll want to go left from there so you don't double back by the cabin."

"Thanks, Chief. We'll be in touch."

"Okay, we have a back way out and we have a contact. What are you going to do about the sketch artist?"

"We're taking him with us. He has a computer and we can use it."

"Any ideas where we will go?"

"Not yet. What about you?" She put the car in gear and they headed for the cabin.

"I'm not sure yet. I might have an idea

CHAPTER NINE

Mark Stone had a source in the department who kept him apprised of what was going on. He had the guy bug Detective Adams car and put a GPS locator on it just in case he needed to know what was going on. He felt safe. He thought maybe he should see what was new on the case. Sgt. Wade Wilson was an over weight, disgruntled cop who spent most of his time on the desk.

The phone rang at the desk of Sgt. Wade Wilson.

"Ridge Cliff Police Department, Wilson."

"Hey, Wade."

"What are you doing calling me here?" Wilson glanced around to see if anyone was listening. Seeing no one he breathed a bit easier.

"Just wondered if Wonder Girl had anything new on her plate."

"She's disappeared."

"She's what? I thought you had a GPS on her car."

"She must have found it and the bug, too. I haven't heard anything since she picked up the kid from arson, Robins. Lost the signal about fifteen minutes later."

"Well, what is she nosing around in?"

Wilson again looked around to see if anyone was nearby then said conspiratorially, "She got the murder of Mike Desmond handed to her. She's been teamed up with the Robins kid from arson to crack the case.

From here it looks more like they are getting chummy rather than solving the case." When he chuckled it had a seedy sound.

Stone was silent for a moment, and then he said, "Let me know if she turns up. I'll be at the diner near the park for dinner around seven if you get anything. If not, I won't see you."

"Sure thing." Wilson hung up the phone and headed for the coffee machine. If there was any gossip it would be found there. He hoped he had something to report at seven. He liked eating at the diner even if Stone did not.

Stone hung up the phone and took a walk toward the park. So, Wonder Girl had someone new and the Homestead case. This could be interesting. He might enjoy playing some cat and mouse with her before he left. He had been using Wilson for information for the past year. Right after the drug bust went bad.

He hated to think about the bust. He had been lead and the information had been good. They busted into the apartment and all there were inside were some frightened illegals. Then someone had planted drugs under the sofa and one of the kids found it and thought it was sugar. It had been awful. The kid died. Stone had been through an Internal Affairs investigation. It was suggested he take some time off.

He took some time alright. He took time and cultivated the people investing in water front property. He had gone to meetings with board chairmen. He had even recorded the meetings and deleted some of the essential parts of the meetings. He had used the parts he kept to blackmail three very important men into giving him very big amounts of money after their buildings burned.

He used the time he had spent with the fire department to hone his skills. When the time was right, the first building went up in smoke. Everyone got out, but they had not been able to save the building. They could not find the arsonist. He smiled. They would never find him.

JAKE CALLED AHEAD and told Mr. Sullivan to start packing up and to pack up any food he could. He explained they would be moving to another location and to see if there was a cooler around they could put perishables in. Then he asked if Rachel could speak to the sketch artist.

"Milt, this is Detective Adams. I want you to listen carefully. We have a situation here. Jake Robins from arson and I are on the way to the cabin. We are going to pick up you and the Sullivans. The photo you sent me is an ex-cop. We have to keep this under wrap. You just became a material witness. Shut down your computer. Gather your stuff and be ready to load up when we get there. Say nothing to upset the Sullivans. Pretend this is routine. Any questions?"

Milt stammered, "Mmmy wife, um won't she worry?"

"Milt, I will have someone contact your wife. It will be fine this is just for a couple of days. You are not going into a dangerous situation; we are going to take you out of one. Is there someplace your wife can go visit for a few days?"

"Her mother?"

"Good idea. We'll have her go there right now. In the meantime, just stay calm."

"Sure, I mean okay."

The call ended and she looked at Jake. "I've got to get his wife out of town. I need to call Lt. Watson. He's as solid as a log."

She began to dial Lt. Watson.

"Watson."

"Lieutenant, Adams here. We have a problem."

"What's now?"

"We have a tentative ID on someone who may be our arsonist. We have an eye witness who puts him at the scene. The problem is my car was bugged and a GPS was mounted on it. We are moving the witness, and I will be out of contact. We also are taking Milt Stephens with us. His wife will have to be sent out of town for her safety. Can you give him a cover and have her go to her mother's?"

"Slow down, let me get this straight. Your car was bugged? Someone was tracking you? Are you telling me our suspect is a cop?" he asked incredulously.

"Our suspect is Mark Stone. I think he has a mole in the department, yes."

"Okay, who all is with you and who else knows?"

"I have Jake Robins from arson and all his files with me; we are going to pick up the Sullivans and Milt. The only other person who knows this is Chief McDonald. He told us how to leave without alerting the cops on duty."

"Okay, I'm going to leave them on duty as if nothing has changed. I'll get with McDonald later. You take care and keep me up to speed. Meanwhile I'm going to turn this department upside down and find a mole. Then I'm going to bury him."

They hung up and Rachel made the turn to the cabin. She stopped to check in with the guys on duty and then they drove the rest of the way to the cabin. Jake directed her as they drove around the back.

When the car stopped Jake hopped out saying, "You start getting things in the trunk I'm going to see if I can find the two track."

Rachel nodded and headed for the cabin. Just like at lunch Lupe was at the door.

"Rachel, you came back."

"Yes, Lupe, and we're going to go to a different place. You, your grandfather, Milt, Jake, and I are going to work on something together."

"Cool."

They went inside. Rachel could tell Milt was uncomfortable. She directed Mr. Sullivan to start taking things out to the car. He nodded and found something for Lupe to carry. Then she walked over to Milt.

Quietly she said, "Milt the Lieutenant has everything under control. This is going to be just a few days of computer work for you."

He nodded and started carrying his computer to the car. He was a sniveling little man very nondescript. Most of the time he went unnoticed in the department, but he was a computer genius. He was at home with computers. People made him nervous.

Jake met Mr. Sullivan and Lupe on their way out to the car. He took the box and began putting things in the trunk. Milt came out and added his computer. They finished loading the car.

Rachel and Milt sat in the front, Jake, Lupe, and Mr. Sullivan sat in the back. Jake told Rachel where to drive, to take a right at the fork and turn left on the main road. Then he settled back into the seat.

Once on the main road, Rachel asked where they should go. Jake thought for a moment then asked for the phone. He made a quick call to a friend from college and then hung up.

"My buddy Matt says his grandfather still has a cabin about twenty miles north of here. We will find the key above the door frame. It's not been used since last hunting season and we are welcome to stay there."

"Great. Point me in the right direction."

Jake quickly gave Rachel the directions.

"This is like a great adventure isn't it?" Lupe asked.

"That it is," Mr. Sullivan replied.

Everyone else was quiet, deep in their own thoughts.

CHAPTER TEN

In Ridge Cliff there were several things going on. Lt. Watson had personally gone to see Milt's wife. She was thrilled to be going to see her mother. He had also called Internal Affairs. He wanted every man and woman in his squad room put under a microscope, especially those who had worked with Mark Stone. Watson was mad and getting ready to clean house. He had also had a phone conversation with Chief McDonald at the fire department.

Wade Wilson had made two or three trips to the coffee machine. He could tell something was going on. A couple of Internal Affairs people had been in to see the Lieutenant; he could tell it had been a heated conversation. He steered clear of the Lieutenant when he was angry. He did not hear anything about Adams though. He wandered by her desk to see if there was anything carelessly left on it which might be of interest. He was disappointed; it was neat as a pin, not a scrap of paper to be found.

Shift change still found him with nothing exciting to report. It seems Internal Affairs was going to be talking to the entire squad. He did wonder what it was about, but didn't give it much thought. It looked like he would miss dinner at the diner. Maybe tomorrow something would turn up. It was then he overheard, "The Lieutenant seems to think someone in the squad is leaking information."

He was instantly on edge. He quickly went to his desk and erased his caller ID for the day. He picked up his jacket and headed out of the building. He had to talk to Stone tonight. He needed to sever all connections until the heat was off. He was too close to pension to get tossed out now

THEY FOUND THE cabin without too much trouble. Milt didn't like being so far from the city. They got everything unloaded and into the cabin. Jake found the gas tank to be half full and turned it on.

It was two bedrooms, a small living room, a kitchen/dining area combined and a bathroom. It was decided Rachel and Lupe would share one room. Milt and Mr. Sullivan would take the other and Jake would take the couch, which to his surprise turned out to be a hide-a-bed.

Rachel started setting up the kitchen. Mr. Sullivan helped. They found a make shift desk in the living area and Milt went to work setting up his computer. Jake went outside and called the Chief.

"McDonald here."

"Chief, it's Jake. We are set up in a hunting cabin belonging to a buddy of mine. We should be ok here."

"Great! Is there anything you need?"

"Just time. Rachel and I are going to start looking through the other fire records and get Milt to put information into his computer looking for patterns or similarities."

"Okay, Jake, keep me posted. I don't like having you out there unprotected."

"Oh, we are protected, Chief. Rachel has her service revolver and I found a couple of rifles and some shells. Mr. Sullivan and I can help defend us, if the need arises."

"If you're sure..."

"I am. Chief, it's better we do it this way. Right now only one person is suspicious."

"Check in regularly and let me know if there is any progress."

"Will do."

Jake pocketed the phone, made one more trip around the place, checked to be sure Rachel's car was out of sight and locked, and then went inside.

The smell of food filled the little cabin. Lupe was busy setting the table. Rachel and Mr. Sullivan were working as a team in the kitchen. Jake went into the bedroom to see how Milt was doing.

Milt jumped when the door squeaked.

"Sorry to startle you."

"No problem. I don't usually get this kind of assignment. It's a bit nerve wracking."

"It is for all of us. Can't say my job has ever been this exciting either," Jake chuckled and then asked, "How are you doing on getting set up?"

"Since there is no phone, I'm set up for non-network stuff. If we need to network, someone is going to have to see if the phone company can get us a temporary set up."

"I don't think we'll be here very long."

"Good."

Lupe appeared in the doorway to tell them dinner was ready. The two men followed the little girl to the dining area.

Lupe kept dinner lively with conversation. The adults were distracted by their own thoughts. After dinner and dishes, Rachel and Jake started going through the fire files one by one. Each made a list of significant things they found. Rachel was slowed a bit by the technical terms for the tests used and their results, but she managed to get through it.

Once they were done they compared lists and discussed what they had each found. They gave the things they both of them found to Milt to enter into the computer as a basis for further study. Then they decided to call it a day. Jake found a flashlight and did a check once more around the perimeter of the cabin. Nothing had changed.

CHAPTER ELEVEN

B ack in Ridge Cliff Wade Wilson made his way to the diner. He had picked a booth in the back and flipped through the sports section while waiting for Stone to show up.

At seven sharp Stone strolled in. He asked the waitress for a coffee and spotted Wilson in the back.

"I'll be joining my friend in the back," he said.

"I'll bring it right over."

He walked to the booth and slid in. Wilson put the newspaper aside. "We got a problem."

"What kind of problem?"

The conversation stopped as the waitress came with a cup of coffee and the pot to refill Wilson's cup.

"Are you ready to order?"

Stone said, "I'll have the special."

Wilson said, "I want the fish and chips with the cole slaw."

"I'll have it out in a minute."

"You can bring the slaw with the meal."

"Sure, whatever you want." She walked back to place their orders.

"Okay, what is this problem?"

"Watson had Internal Affairs people in his office today. It was a heated discussion. Later I heard he is looking for some kind of mole. Have you done something I might take the fall for?"

"You know Watson; he's always on some kind of crusade."

"Yeah, but I don't know what you're into these days."

"Security advisor, nothing special. In fact, in a couple of days I'll be relocating. So, you can rest easy."

"Relocating? Some place outside the city?"

"Some place outside the country."

"This must be some cushy job. Do they have any openings?"

"Not at the moment, but I'll mention your name."

"Thanks, Stone."

"So, did Wonder Girl reappear? Do you think she took a long week-end with the arson guy?"

"As far as I can tell that's what happened. No one has asked about her and no one is looking for her." Wilson paused a moment then said, "Something must be up."

"What makes you say so?"

"Do you know anyone who just takes off in the middle of a case where a cop is killed?"

"Hmm it's something to ponder. You've done well today. I'll buy dinner and you'll find a substantial reward in your mailbox."

"Thanks, Stone."

"I need you to keep listening. We'll meet for lunch at the deli south of the Ridge Cliff Ledger offices."

"Okay."

"If you have no information, don't show. Otherwise take a late lunch and be there at one."

The waitress returned with their orders and they stopped talking to concentrate on eating. When they were done, Wilson left first while Stone paid the bill. He left and looked both ways. Wilson was no where to be seen. He headed through the park circling twice before going back to his room. He was going to have to think about what to do with Wilson.

JAKE AWOKE EARLY, started coffee, and took a walk around the perimeter of the cabin. When he returned he found Mr. Sullivan in the kitchen.

"Mr. Sullivan, you should take it easy."

"Call me Pat please. I've always been an early riser and the smell of coffee was too tempting to pass up."

"Okay, Pat, but let me make breakfast. Then we'll make a list of the things we need from the store."

By the time breakfast was ready, everyone had gathered in the kitchen and Pat had a list of things they would need to tide them over for the next couple of days. Since Jake knew the area, he was elected to do the shopping. He offered to take Lupe with him.

"Do you think it's wise?" Rachel asked.

"No one knows we're here and there is a little county store about five miles from here. We can be just passing through. I might find something to pick up which will give her something to do."

"Sounds like you've given it some thought."

"Yep, I did."

It was settled Jake and Lupe set out for the store.

Pat and Rachel did the dishes. Milt continued loading the information he had gotten from Rachel and Jake last night. When the dishes were done, Rachel said she was going to take a walk. Pat asked if he could go with her.

"Sure, I'd love the company. I don't get into the woods often and I like the peacefulness of it."

The two of them let Milt know where they were going and set off behind the cabin. Milt got another cup of coffee and continued to work. He was not comfortable in the out of doors. If the truth be told, he was not comfortable with this entire situation. He wished he had taken his cell phone out of his car before they left. They needed more than one cell phone out here.

Meanwhile, Jake and Lupe were having a grand time. When the store owner asked how old his daughter was, Lupe piped up, "I'm six, but this is my big brother Jake, my daddy died."

"I'm so sorry, little Lady," he said and offered her a cinnamon stick.

"Can I, Jake?" she asked.

"Sure, little one."

She reached for the candy and said, "Thank you."

"You're quite welcome."

Jake set their purchases on the counter. "I think this will do it."

The owner rang up the purchases. Jake paid the bill and they left. To be sure they were not followed Jake headed south then cut back on an old trail road not often used. Once he had circled the store and cottages around it, he headed back to the cabin. The entire trip took less than an hour.

When they reached the cabin Pat and Rachel were just returning from their walk. They helped carry the supplies inside. Lupe found a corner and sat down with some paper dolls and coloring books Jake had purchased.

Milt did not appear when they came in. Rachel went to see what he was doing. Milt was lying on the bed sound asleep. She covered him with a blanket and closed the door.

"Where's Milt?" Jake asked.

"Shhh. He's sound asleep. I think this cloak and dagger as you call it is too much for him."

"You're probably right. Shall we tackle the next file?"

They agreed and set to work on the second set of files.

CHAPTER TWELVE

L t. Watson was learning quite a bit about his staff. Internal Affairs had run bank accounts, credit checks and any other financial thing it could to access whether anyone had suspicious spending habits, or wealth hidden away. So far they had turned up nothing out of the ordinary. His cops were not dirty in the sense they were taking payoffs.

Internal Affairs was busy running checks now on anyone who had worked in the department at the same time as Mark Stone.

Watson was really puzzled. He thought he knew his officers. He believed he could count on all of them. He was startled to hear his phone ring.

"Watson."

"This is Chief McDonald. I think we should have lunch together."

"I think you're right. Name the place."

"South of town is a little out of the way Mexican place called Mama Mia."

"I know the place what time?"

"Say one-thirty after the lunch crowd."

"I'll be there."

He hung up the phone and wondered for the first time if maybe the mole was in the fire department. He picked up the phone and called McDonald back.

"McDonald."

"Watson. Do you know where Robins' car is?"

"Yeah, it's an older model Jeep Cherokee parked in the lot here."

"I'm coming over meet me in the lot."

"I'll be there."

The two men hung up and Watson headed out of his office. It took him less than ten minutes to make it across town to the fire department headquarters. Chief McDonald was standing next to a black Jeep Cherokee.

"What's the problem?" the Chief asked.

Watson motioned the Chief to step away from the car. He took a small black box from his pocket and walked around the Jeep. Sure enough there was a GPS tracking device on it. Watson motioned for the Chief and showed him what he had found. They jimmied the locks on the car and Watson did a similar sweep of the car. There were no bugs.

"What does it mean?" asked the Chief.

"I was hoping there wouldn't be anything on this car. Meaning the only mole was in my department. The fact there is no listening device could mean we both have moles."

"Couldn't it mean there is one mole and there wasn't time to install a listening device?"

"Could."

The Chief was puzzled. "Why on earth is someone tracking our people?"

"Could be the weapons we confiscated. Could be the fires, or it could be Desmond's murder."

"That's a lot of could be's."

"Too many and it's getting to be very puzzling."

"I'll say," said the Chief. "What are we going to do about it?"

"Think for a while then meet for lunch as planned. Meantime we're leaving this alone," he said nodding toward the GPS module.

The two men walked away each deep in his own thoughts.

FROM A DISTANCE, Mark Stone watched as the two men walked away from Robins' Jeep. He wondered what they were thinking. He had not had time to place a listening device in the car, but the GPS tracker was enough to throw them off track.

McDonald had not been the Chief when he was there. He had just been the new rising star. He had resented Stone from the first. Now Stone had made him doubt his own staff. It was a small thing, but it was enough to get even for now.

He waited a few minutes then hailed a taxi and rode back to the park. At the east entrance to the park he looked both ways, then strolled through and turned left. He walked two blocks south before circling the block and heading back to his room. There was no sense in getting careless at this late date.

An hour would see him in the deli. Maybe Wilson would show and maybe not.

Wilson showed up. All he could tell Stone was Watson was taking a long lunch.

"So, why does it make any difference?"

"He rarely takes half an hour for lunch. Today he told his secretary he'd be gone a couple of hours."

"Good, I have a plan." He went on to detail his idea for Wilson. The two left ten minutes later.

CHAPTER THIRTEEN

Milt woke just before lunch. He apologized for having slept the morning away. Rachel told him it was nothing and asked if he was ready for the next batch of information.

"I'm ready as soon as you have it," he replied still feeling sheepish.

"Great! I'll give it to you right after lunch."

They ate a meal of sandwiches and salad, then Milt went to work on the computer, and Pat and Jake took Lupe to go fishing in a stream Pat had found earlier.

Left on her own, Rachel cleared away the lunch clutter then stepped outside to call Lt. Watson.

"Watson."

"Hi, Lieutenant, it's Adams."

"Hold on just one moment." He put her on hold and buzzed the department operator.

"Don't put any more calls through to me until further notice."

"Fine, Lieutenant."

Back on the line with Adams he said, "Have you come up with anything?"

"Not yet. Milt is putting in the information we took from the second fire."

"It should help. You'll want to know Robins car has a GPS tracker on it, too."

"Does it mean the mole is in the fire department?"

"It doesn't seem likely, but McDonald is probably checking."

"Lieutenant, we need the files in Jake's apartment. I haven't told him yet, but we are coming in after dark."

"You think it's a good idea?"

"As long as no one knows where we are, we should be okay."

"Alright, check with me once you've been here and gone."

"I will. I guess it means we don't pick up Robins' Jeep."

"Sure you can. The tracker is under the rear passenger wheel. Stick it on something is likely to move."

"Thanks, Lieutenant."

They disconnected. Rachel wandered to where the trio had gone fishing. She needed to tell Jake what they were going to be doing later.

CHIEF MCDONALD SPENT the rest of the morning finding all he could on the time Mark Stone was the police liaison with the department. He remembered Stone vividly.

The man was tall with dark hair and eyes almost black. He dressed in a suit and thought he was the lord of all he met. He seemed keenly interested in how fires started. It was almost as if he were obsessed with them. Most of the time, he just got in the way. McDonald had been glad when Stone was called back to work a narcotics bust.

There was a knock on his door.

"Come in."

His secretary entered and brought him a file.

"Thank you. I'll be leaving the building for a late lunch today."

"Sure, Chief," she replied as she left the room.

McDonald opened the file. There was a photo of Stone staring back at him. The look on his face was almost insolent. He quickly read through the file. There did not seem to be much in it. Stone had kept his nose clean while he was there. He would take it to lunch anyway. Maybe Watson would see something he missed.

An hour later he left his office. Stopping at his secretary's desk he said, "Use my cell if something urgent comes up, otherwise I'll be gone for a couple of hours."

"Sure thing," she responded.

Then he walked away.

Strange she thought. Chief McDonald rarely took an half an hour for lunch much less two. She would not worry about it; he was a nice man to work for and she liked the job.

RACHEL FOLLOWED THE sound of laughter until she came upon her trio of fishermen. They were splashing in the stream.

Lupe, who was sitting on the bank, saw her first and called, "Come on, Rachel."

Rachel laughed. "Not right now, Lupe. I need to talk to Jake. I thought you guys were fishing."

Pat raised his arm and held aloft a line full of fish.

"We're giving the fish a break."

"I see. Can I expect fresh fish for dinner?"

"You sure can. We found a grill in the old shed and some charcoal."

"Sounds delicious."

Jake made his way to the creek bank. "What's up? Did Milt find something?"

"I don't know he was busy working when I left. There is something else we need to talk about."

"Okay, let's go this way," he said heading off on a trail away from the cabin."

They waved to Pat and Lupe and said they'd be back shortly. Once out of ear shot Rachel stopped.

"Jake, your car also has a GPS tracker on it. Is there anyone you can think of in the fire department who might have an interest in this case?"

"No, I haven't ever had a problem with anyone. No one has even asked me about the case?" Jake frowned. "So, do you have any other good news?"

Rachel smiled. "Yep, we're going into enemy territory tonight."

Jake looked at her skeptically and asked, "Would you care to explain?"

"We need another car. We also need the case files in your apartment. So, we are going into Ridge Cliff under cover of darkness. We're going to put the GPS tracker from your car onto someone else's and we're going to get the files from your apartment. Any questions?"

"You make it sound like a prank," he said seriously.

"Well, it's not a prank. We have to get in and out of town without anyone knowing we are there. We don't want to tip off whoever is trying to track us."

"You're right. What are we going to tell the others?"

"We're only going to tell Pat."

Jake was puzzled, "Why not tell Milt?"

"This is so far out of what Milt is used to I think it would send him over the edge."

"Okay, what do you say we head back?"

She laughed and started running back down the path. "Catch me if you can," she yelled over her shoulder.

Jake turned quickly and started running. His soggy shoes slowed him down a bit. He caught her by the time they reached the creek. Without thinking he grabbed her and threw her into the water.

She let out a whoop as she struggled to get up. Jake jumped in and helped her. In his efforts to lend a hand he found himself face first in the water. Rachel stood laughing as he dragged himself back up. The two of them walked to the bank and headed back to the cabin hand in hand. To Jake it just seemed right.

MCDONALD AND WATSON met in the parking lot of Mama Mia at one. They walked in and found a booth in the small section of the restaurant off the main room. The waitress came to take their drink orders. When both men asked for Coke she sensed they wanted privacy and offered to bring them a pitcher. They thanked her.

When she walked away, McDonald asked, "Do you want to order first then talk?"

"Sounds like a good idea."

They studied the menu and were ready to order when the waitress came back with their drinks. Watson ordered a trio of enchiladas smothered in sauce and rice. McDonald ordered grilled chicken fajitas with the works. The waitress told them it would be right out. Both men began eating chips and salsa.

Watson spoke first. "I still think the mole is in the police department. Stone wasn't in the fire department long enough to make many close friends."

"I don't recall he made any," said McDonald, "and you're right it wasn't long only about eight months."

"What do you know about him?"

McDonald handed Watson the file as he spoke, "He gave me the creeps. He was always trying to find out how to start fires. It seemed like he was obsessed with knowing different ways to start a fire. It just struck me as odd."

"Not much here," said Watson. "He thought he was a go getter in the squad. He came in dressed like he was a ladies man and tried to muscle in on everyone's case, especially if he thought he'd get press from it."

"Well, there is plenty of reason to put him on the suspect list."

"Coupled with the fact no one has seen him for a while either."

They paused as the waitress put down their food. Then it was silent as each man began to eat his lunch.

Midway through the meal, McDonald asked, "What have you found out about the weapons? Could Stone have been involved in it?"

"I don't think so. Adams is going to retrieve the case notes from Desmond's partner tonight."

"Where are the case notes?"

"They left them in Robin's apartment. They'd had plans to continue working on them last night."

"They're coming into town?" McDonald choked out.

"Calm down. They aren't coming in until after dark. I gave Adams orders to call me when they were back to safety. You should also know Robins' Jeep will be gone in the morning. They are going to put the GPS tracker on some other vehicle."

"Sounds like you have it all worked out. Why wasn't I told?"

"It came about after we talked this morning. I don't even think Robins' knew at the time. I said I would inform you."

"Okay."

They enjoyed the rest of their meal and chatted about family and friends they had in common. Both men left feeling like they knew each other better, but with each having their own concerns about the case.

CHAPTER FOURTEEN

P at standing at the grill saw them coming back from the river and sent Lupe to get them towels. He raised his hand to wave.

Rachel dropped Jake's hand self-consciously. She whispered, "I'll keep Lupe occupied, you tell Pat about the plan for tonight."

"Sounds good."

Lupe emerged with two towels and handed one to each of them.

"Lupe, you want to come and help me out?" Rachel asked.

"Okay," she said as she scampered behind Rachel as quickly as her clumsy gait allowed her to move.

While drying himself somewhat, Jake walked toward Pat.

"Rachel and I need some files from my apartment," Jake said simply.

"How do you plan to get them?"

"We are going into town around midnight. We'll pick up my Jeep so we have an extra vehicle and then go to my place. With luck we should be back here by three."

"Will Milt be going too?"

"No, we're not even telling him. This cloak and dagger stuff has him wired enough."

"I can keep it under my hat. What's so important about this file?"

"It will help us know what Officer Desmond was doing in your building."

Lupe had come out and was within hearing distance. "Mr. Mike kept a book in the secret place," she said.

Startled both Pat and Jake looked at her. Jake recovered first and asked, "What secret place, Lupe?"

Just then Rachel appeared, "Did I hear someone has a secret?"

Jake responded, "It seems our Officer Desmond kept a book in a secret place."

"Lupe, do you know where this secret place is?" Rachel asked.

"Yes."

"Can you tell us?"

"It's hard to tell you but I can draw a picture."

Rachel held out her hand to Lupe, "Come on let's get a picture drawn."

The two of them headed toward the cabin. Jake and Pat just stood there. Finally Pat said, "You'd better get yourself into dry clothes."

Jake nodded and headed inside, too. After a dinner of grilled fish, Milt asked Jake and Rachel to look at what he had found after entering their information. The pattern showed the first two fires were started with matches and a cigarette and set in gasoline. A burned out match book and cigarette butt were found at the scene. They knew how the first two fires were started.

"Milt, do you want to help us go through the third file? You know what to look for now."

"I'd love to. Then I don't have to think about being isolated out here with nothing to do," he replied. The three of them sat at the kitchen table with the file from the third fire. They worked until about nine-thirty then Rachel stretched.

"I think I'm going to head for bed and work on this tomorrow."

Jake nodded and said, "I think I'm going to turn in too."

Milt looked up. "Jake will it bother you if I work on this a little longer?"

"No, I'll just roll away from the light."

"I can sit over in the corner. The light is not as bright there."

"Thanks." Jake pulled out the bed and turned in.

Milt moved to the other side of the room with the files.

In the bedroom she shared with Lupe, Rachel set the alarm on her watch. She hoped Milt would be fast asleep by eleven-thirty.

IN HIS OFFICE Lt. Watson paced. He was wondering who he could trust. He wanted to know everything there was to know about the weapons they had confiscated and the people who might be moving weapons. Ridge Cliff was not a big town. He stopped his pacing and looked out on the squad room.

There were several people working at their desks. Some were more nervous today than usual. Word of the Internal Affairs investigation had spread quickly. There had to be someone. He wondered who Adams would pick. Then he reached for the phone to call her. He stopped mid-way through the number when his other line lit up.

"Lt. Watson." He could hear someone breathing on the other line. "Hello, you've reached Lt. Watson of the Ridge Cliff Police Department. How can I help you?"

Still silence, then the line went dead. He stood there holding it for a minute then hung it up and buzzed his secretary. "Who was on the call you just put through?"

"I didn't put a call through, Lieutenant. It must have come from someone internally. Why?"

"No reason. Thanks."

Now he was really puzzled. Again he looked out at his squad. Someone out there knows something. He sat at his desk and unscrewed the mouth piece of his phone. Sure enough, there was a bug. This was too much.

He walked to his secretary's desk and said, "Get someone from Internal Affairs up here now." Then he turned on his heel and went back into his office slamming the door. He wondered how long the bug had been there. Was Adams in jeopardy?

The internal affairs office sent someone right away. Lt. Watson escorted the man to his office.

"Davis I want you to see something," he said without ceremony. Then he carefully lifted the mouth piece from his phone.

Davis whistled. "I'll get fingerprint up here right now."

"Ask my secretary to call them. I don't know how long this has been here, but I do know I may have an officer compromised."

"Lieutenant, my staff will be crawling all over this squad room is less than thirty minutes. No one is to leave."

The chief walked out of his office and into the squad room. "I need to make an announcement. As of this minute no one is to leave the squad room."

A chorus of 'Aws' could be heard throughout the room. Someone said, "It's dinner time."

"I'll have pizza ordered in on the department," Watson said. He nodded to his secretary who nodded back. As soon as Davis was done with the phone she ordered the pizzas.

In Watson's office, Davis said, "I have staff on the way. We'll set up in the interrogation rooms and conference rooms."

"You can use my office as soon as finger print is done. I need to leave the building and try to contact my field officer. She needs to know she may be compromised."

Davis nodded. His staff was coming off the elevator now. He walked out and began setting up for investigation.

Wade Wilson also watched. He saw the Lieutenant leave and he saw the invasion of the Internal Affairs staff. He wondered if he had gone too far this time.

Outside Watson dialed Chief McDonald.

"McDonald."

"Watson, take down this number walk outside and call it on your cell phone."

"Okay."

Watson paced outside as he waited for McDonald to call him back. He jumped when the phone rang.

"Watson."

"What's going on?"

"My office phone was bugged. I don't think yours is, but I didn't want to take a chance. I'm going to call Adams in case she's been compromised. I just wanted you to know."

"Thanks for the heads up. You have my cell number, use it from now on."

Both men rang off. McDonald headed back to his office prepared to take his phone apart. He didn't want to have a traitor in his department.

Watson dialed the cell number Adams had given him. He got the voice mail. "Adams, I need you to call me as soon as you get this. You may have been compromised."

He had done all he could, now he would go see what Internal Affairs found.

Davis watched him come in. As soon as Watson had reached his office door, he knew they had found his mole.

"Spit it out."

"Fingerprint came back and the ones on the bug belonged to Mark Stone and Wade Wilson."

"Wilson," Watson hissed. "I didn't think he had the gumption to do something like this."

"Well, evidently you were wrong. We went back and looked carefully into him."

"Let me have it."

"He seems to be coming into unexplained money. Not large amounts, but they've been steady for about eight months."

"Which would be about the time Stone dropped out of sight."

"Makes sense. What are you going to do?"

"Give me everything you have. We're either going to scare him to death or arrest him for obstruction of justice," Watson said. "Either way he's finished in the department."

CHAPTER FIFTEEN

Milt was just nodding off when he thought he heard a sound. He listened quietly for a moment. Then he heard the sound of a car. He almost fell trying to get out of the bed.

Pat who had heard Milt come in said, "What is it Milt?"

"Hush, you fool! I heard something out there and a car just drove off."

"Of course it did," Pat replied, "Jake and Rachel are leaving." He reached up and turned on the light.

"Leaving!" Milt bellowed.

"Yes, they have to go into town."

"And you knew about this?"

"Yes."

"Why on earth didn't they tell me?"

Pat sat up and looked at the little man. "I don't rightly know," he said.

"Did they tell you why they were going?"

"I can't recall. Why don't you get back in bed and go to sleep?"

Milt pouted for a moment. He had not asked to be a part of this mess. Then he climbed into bed.

"If it's any consolation, I didn't ask to be part of it either," Pat said.

"I know."

"Good night," said Pat as he turned off the light.

ONCE THEY HAD cleared the cabin, Rachel took out the cell phone and turned it on. She plugged it into the battery charger and into the cigarette lighter in the car. The phone face lit up and it gave an agitated beep.

"What on earth?" Jake said.

"Looks like we have a message. Hand me the phone and I'll see what it is." Rachel dialed a couple of numbers and listened to Lt. Watson tell her they might be compromised. "Pull over."

"What is it?"

"The lieutenant. He thinks we might be in danger. Let me call him." She dialed the lieutenant's cell phone number.

Watson was asleep in his favorite chair. His wife had draped a blanket over him. He heard the sound of his cell phone.

"Watson," he said sleepily.

"Lieutenant, this is Adams. How have we been compromised?"

Instantly alert he answered, "We found the mole. He didn't plant the phone bug until after we had talked. You are good to go, just be careful. We've put a BOLO out for Mark Stone. No one is to approach him yet."

"Okay, we're on our way in. We'll call when we are clear of town."

"Roger out."

She clicked the phone shut and looked at Jake. "We're okay. They found the mole in the department and the lieutenant has put a BOLO out on Mark Stone."

"What's a BOLO?"

"Be on the lookout," she said smiling. "They are looking for him, but will not apprehend him yet."

Jake started the car and they headed toward town. They made good time as there was little traffic. The first stop was to pick up Jake's Jeep. Rachel took the GPS tracker and attached it to a car parked on the street.

"Okay, I'm going to my apartment. I'm going to get the file and grab some clothes. I think I might have a pair of jeans and a shirt Milt can wear."

"How would you have something so small?"

"It would be left from the last time my brother came to visit."

"Okay, then I will go to my apartment and grab some clothes. Where do you want to meet?"

"There's an all night restaurant at the cross roads north of town."

"Sounds good, you only have an hour."

"Plenty of time. See you then."

Each got into their car and drove off. Adams circled the area twice before heading to her apartment. Jake took a circuitous route to his apartment.

Forty-five minutes later he pulled into the all night restaurant to wait for Rachel. He was surprised to see Mark Stone pull in a few minutes later. He got out of his car and walked into the restaurant. Jake saw Stone make his way to the back of the restaurant. He wished he had a cell phone. Just then Rachel pulled in. She pulled her car next to Jake's.

Jake got out and told her they needed to get out of there. Mark Stone was inside.

Rachel grabbed the cell and called Lt. Watson.

"Watson."

"Lieutenant, it's Rachel. We're at the all night diner at the cross roads. Stone just showed up."

"Get out of there! I'll send someone to keep an eye on him."

"Leaving now." She hung up and looked at Jake.

He returned to his car and they both drove away. Rachel followed him. He took a different route than before. Both of them were watching their rear view mirrors to see if they had a tail. They did not and returned to the cabin at two-thirty, an hour ahead of schedule.

They entered quietly only to find Milt and Pat in the kitchen having coffee. They joined them at the table to talk about the night. Jake offered the extra set of clothes to Milt and everyone settled into bed.

LT. WATSON CALLED dispatch and sent them to the all night diner. He wanted them to tail Stone. He didn't want them to apprehend him or give chase, just follow him. Then report to Watson at the end of their shift.

Having the crisis settled he made some coffee and went back to his favorite chair. It wasn't long before Adams called in.

"Watson."

"Adams, we've made it back."

"Good, get some sleep and let me know what you find." Then he asked as an after thought, "Adams, who in the department would you want watching your back?"

She thought for a minute then said, "Alan Bosworth."

"Good choice. I'm going to be putting him on the job of tracing those weapons."

"Night, Lieutenant."

"Night."

He couldn't go back to sleep, so he turned on the all night movie channel and settled in with a war movie. 'The Guns of Navarone' was playing. In less than half an hour he was asleep.

CHAPTER SIXTEEN

The detail assigned to tail Stone called for an unmarked back up team then entered the diner. The two uniformed cops took seats at a booth near the door.

Wilson had seen them come in. "Uniforms up front."

"Great. You stop and talk to them I'll pay the bill and slip out."

"Got your back." Wilson got up and moved to the front of the diner. He stopped and stood next to the table where the two uniformed officers were having coffee.

"Rough night?" he asked casually.

"Pretty quiet," one responded. "Do you need something, Sir?"

"Wilson, homicide."

"Didn't I hear something about you today?"

"Yeah," he said sheepishly. "I retired."

"Congratulations!" Both men reached to shake his hand. At the same time, Stone walked out the front door and headed away from the diner.

Wilson continued with inconsequential chat for about five more minutes then headed for his car.

Stone doubled back about two blocks from the diner and headed in a different direction. He entered the park from the east and exited going south. He then found an alley and doubled back. He entered his building from the alley.

The detail following him lost him in the alley. They were going to take some heat in the morning for losing him.

LUPE WAS UP before everyone. She occupied herself coloring at the table. Her soft humming woke Jake.

"Good morning, Sunshine."

"Shh! Good morning," she whispered. "No one else is up yet."

"Well, give me a minute and I'll make some breakfast." He was glad for the forethought which made him grab his bath robe. He threw it on before getting out of the bed. He went to the bathroom, then to the kitchen to start coffee and breakfast.

Rachel was the next one to make an appearance. "Don't you look at home," she said with a chuckle.

"You didn't have an audience this morning or you'd be in your robe too."

"Coffee smells great!"

He poured her a cup. "Hope you like flap jacks."

"What are flap jacks?" Lupe wanted to know.

"It's just a different way to say pancakes," Rachel assured her. "I found some blueberries and added them to the mix."

"Sounds good. Lupe, shall we set the table?"

While the two of them set the table for breakfast, they were joined by Pat. As they were sitting down to eat, Milt arrived, looking more relaxed and comfortable in the jeans and shirt Jake had found for him.

As the table talk slowed, Milt said, "I found something in the three fires I'd like you to look at."

"As soon as we're done," Rachel replied.

After breakfast, Pat and Lupe cleaned up while Rachel, Jake, and Milt went to look at Milt's computer.

"It seems the same accelerant was used in all the fires. It was gasoline. In all three of the first fires a book of burned matches was believed to be the starter," he said.

"It wasn't?" Jake asked.

"No, it seems it was used as a back up."

"Can you explain this to me?" Rachel asked.

"Sure, in each of the fires there was a line from the detonation point to the burn center. There was also a secondary line," Milt replied.

"We've just found the incendiary devices for the secondary lines." Jake said.

"Now you've got it!"

"I found a burned out match book, too."

"Great! The same person set all four fires."

"And we have reason to believe we know who the person is, but we can't prove it," said Rachel.

"Do you have the cigarette butts from the match books?" Milt asked.

"I have the one from the last fire. Why?"

"You should also have DNA on the cigarette butt."

"Milt, you are a genius! I need to get back to my lab."

"Wait a minute, hold on!" said Rachel, "I hate to burst your bubble, but you cannot go back to the lab right now."

"So, how soon can I? Does the department have DNA on file for Stone? If not, we can get it when he is arrested."

"Slow down. I need to think. We still need some kind of motive."

"If we can get his bank records maybe he's been paid to burn the buildings," Milt said.

Rachel walked out of the room.

"What's with her?" Milt asked.

"There is a leak in the department, it's why we're here in the first place," Jake replied. "It's why we have to be careful."

"I'm glad you trusted me," Milt said.

"We really didn't feel we had any choice," Jake said sadly.

"I know."

"Did you recognize the man Lupe had you draw?"

"No, he was long gone from the department when I arrived."

"It's probably why Rachel didn't suspect you."

"I'm hardly one to work behind someone's back."

"I think we know, Milt," Rachel said from the doorway. "Jake, is there anyone in your lab you trust to complete your tests?"

"Sure there are several capable people in the lab."

"No, just one person who can cover your back?"

"Yeah, I'm sure there is one person I can trust. What do you have in mind?"

"I want to put Stone on notice. We need someone who can pull DNA and see if there are any cigarette butts from the first fires and pull DNA. I want to be sure it's the same person. Then I want the task force to make a joint statement we have the DNA."

"Are you nuts? It would give away everything we have."

"Not everything. We do have an eye witness."

"Ok, you want to take the heat off Lupe."

"More or less. I also want to rattle Stone."

"Where does it leave me?" Milt asked.

"As far as I'm concerned you can go back to work as normal," Rachel said. "And Milt, you've been a great sport through all this."

"Thanks."

Rachel went on to detail the plan to the two men. They would leave her car with Pat and Lupe. She had to call the Lieutenant and see what he said, but she thought they had enough to be safe. Then they pooled the money the three of them had to leave with Pat and Lupe for supplies.

Jake, Pat and Lupe went fishing while Rachel made her call and Milt picked up his computer and put all the files together.

"So, you'll be leaving us for a while?" asked Pat.

"Yes, we've got some money so you can get supplies and we're giving you Rachel's car to use."

"You'll be safe?"

"We will, we just want to make sure you and Lupe are."

"I appreciate it."

"You have been through a lot," Jake said, "and Lupe has been a great help. No one knows where you are so there shouldn't be any problem." "And your friend, who owns the cabin?"

"I'll call him when we are away and let him know it is going to be in use for a while. It shouldn't be a problem, they only come up during hunting season and it's a good four months away."

"Thank you."

Jake reached out to shake hands with Pat and found himself in a big hug from the older man.

"Lupe, come here please," her grandfather called.

Lupe bounced awkwardly over to the two men.

"Lupe, Rachel, Milt and I are leaving today. We won't be back for a while. You need to stay close to the cabin and don't go wandering without your grandfather." Jake told her seriously.

"Okay, Jake," she said smiling up at him. "You will bring Rachel back again won't you?"

"You bet I will."

They walked back to the cabin together. Lupe went ahead when the cabin came into view.

"Rachel," she called.

Rachel came around the cabin and Lupe flew into her arms.

"I'm going to miss you," she said.

"I'm going to miss you, too."

"I have a picture of where the secret book is in the basement," Lupe said and ran to where she had her paper and crayons. She looked through them, found one and handed it to Rachel. "There's where Mr. Mike put the secret book."

"Thank you, Sweetie."

Rachel, Milt and Jake got into Jake's Jeep and drove away. Pat and Lupe stood waving until they were gone from sight.

"Well, young lady, it's just the two of us."

"It's okay, Papa," she said as she took his hand, "we'll be just fine."

He nodded and said, "Yes, I think we will." Together they went into the cabin to finish cleaning up. On the table Pat found an envelope containing $125 and a note saying use whatever you need the car has almost a full tank of gas. Go right out the driveway and the store is about four miles up the road on the left. One of us will be back as soon as we can.

CHAPTER SEVENTEEN

J
ake went into the Chief's cabin by the back. Milt got out and went to his car. He drove out the front as Rachel and Jake drove out the back. The two officers waved to Milt as he left.

Rachel called the lieutenant and asked him to have Bosworth get in touch with her right away.

Then they quietly drove back to town. They headed for the Homestead. They wanted to find the secret book before anyone else did. There were two officers still on duty there.

The cell phone rang just as they pulled in.

"Adams."

"This is Bos. You need me for something?"

"Yeah, meet me at the Homestead."

"How soon?"

"Now would be good." She hung up the phone and told the men Sergeant Bosworth would be here soon to tell him they were in the back. Then they headed to the basement.

Once inside, they turned on their flashlights and headed for the underground tunnels. Armed with Lupe's map they started looking for the secret book. They had been at it about ten minutes when they heard a roar.

"What on earth?"

Rachel smiled, "Bos making an entrance." She walked toward the opening and yelled, "Down here, Bos."

A lumbering giant appeared above her. Alan Bosworth was close to six foot six and built like a line backer. He grinned when he saw her, his smile lighting up his entire face.

"What's a nice girl like you doin' down there?"

"Looking for Desmond's secret journal. Care to help?"

"Comin' right down." He switched on his flashlight and maneuvered his hulk down the stairs.

"I think I've found something," Jake called.

The two made their way by flashlight to where he was standing. Jake looked up when his light was blocked by the hulking shape of Sgt. Bosworth. Rachel quickly made introductions.

"I could use a hand here," Jake said. "It seems this cinder block is loose, but I cannot get it to come out."

"Stand aside. I think I can handle this."

Jake stepped aside and Bosworth moved in to remove the block. Within seconds he had freed the block. All lights shone into the cavity left there. Sitting behind the block was a battered black notebook.

"I believe this is the secret book," said Rachel stating the obvious.

"Well, pull it out and let's see if it was worth the work."

She reached in to take out the notebook. They all went back up the stairs to see what they had found.

They walked silently back to the cars. Each waved to the duty officers. Jake suggested they go some place and read the journal. Bosworth offered his place. It was agreed. Jake followed Rachel and Bosworth in his Jeep.

STONE HAPPENED TO glance out the window of his room as the three were returning to their cars. It appeared they had something with them. He wondered what they had found.

Tonight he thought he would see if he could get into the Homestead. He really wanted to look at what the fired had done.

He would take coffee and sandwiches to the patrolmen on the graveyard shift an old trick which might get him a look and some information. He had been able to do some schmoozing when he was on the force. He probably had not lost his touch. Maybe he could pretend to be a reporter or a private investigator. He would think of something. He would also work on a disguise.

Now he had something to plan he would have something useful to do for the afternoon. He went to his closet and rummaged through looking for the right clothes for his evening excursion.

MILT MADE HIS way home. Took a long hot shower and found some of his own clothes to put on. He called the office and told them he would be in first thing in the morning.

Then he called his wife at her mother's. He told her he was home and would be back on his regular schedule in the morning. They agreed she would stay through the week-end then return home.

Finally with time on his hands, he opened his laptop and pulled up the data he had entered while in the cabin. He knew there was something he had missed. He could just feel it.

For the first time, he felt like a real police officer. He had been given a task which had taken him away from his desk. He had been put in mortal danger and knew he could survive. Now he wanted to show he had investigative skills, too. He sat down and started looking at all the data again. As he looked he made notes on a sheet of paper next to him. If there was something here he would find it.

He was getting up for his second pot of coffee when he saw what he was looking for. He let out a whoop. It had to do with the security company. He would check one more thing then make a phone call. He knew he had done it. He had found the link.

82

CHAPTER EIGHTEEN

J ake, Rachel, and Bosworth entered Bosworth's small apartment. From the looks of things it had not been cleaned in days.

"Give me a minute to clean the table," he said. "I wasn't expectin' comp'ny."

"No problem, Bos," Rachel replied.

Jake said nothing as he stood there, feeling like an outsider.

Bos quickly had the table cleaned and coffee on.

"Let's look at what we got."

They spread the notebook out on the table. It appeared to be a daily log or journal of Desmond's activities.

Bos got the coffee as Rachel and Jake read.

"Wow!" Jake exclaimed. "He'd found a lot more than he bargained for."

"He sure did," Rachel agreed.

"Let me in on it," said Bos.

"It looks like Desmond stumbled onto the gun runners by accident."

"Figures, the boy couldn't keep out of trouble."

"They seemed to find him harmless, so he must have played his part well," said Jake.

"Desmond could blend in anywhere," said Bos. "It's what made him a good undercover cop."

"He seems to have hit a snag about a week before he died."

"I'd say," said Rachel. "Bos, what do you know about Ike Howser?"

"Ike Howser how does he fit in?"

"Who is Ike Howser?"

"Ike Howser was the contact Desmond had in the department," Rachel explained.

"Howser is really Isaac Horowitz."

"So, what does are you telling me?" Jake asked.

"Isaac Horowitz changed his name to Ike Howser hoping to lose his Jewish background on the force. Someone found out about the name change and he took a lot of razzing."

"What difference does it make if he changed his name?" Jake wanted to know.

"Until now I didn't think it made any difference at all," Rachel said.

"What's different now?"

"Ike was one of the gun runners. He must have stumbled onto Desmond."

"Wouldn't he have known what Desmond was doing?" Jake asked incredulously.

"It seems when Desmond went under no one knew exactly what he was doing or where he was. It was part of his cover and it kept him from being ratted out," said Bos. "Rachel, are you sure Ike was a gun runner?"

"You read it and see what you make of this entry," she said handing the notebook to Bos.

"Maybe he was working the gun case from a different angle."

"I'll check with my sources and see if they had something going on the guns," said Bos. "Meantime, we need to keep this between the three of us until we know exactly what was going on."

"I agree," said Rachel. "We have an eye witness to the murder and it was done by Mark Stone. We have to find a way to tie Stone to Howser before we bust this wide open.

"Okay with me," said Jake. "I'm heading for my place. I want a hot shower and a good night's sleep. Then I'll run the DNA at the lab."

Having decided what next the three split up and went their separate way.

84

MILT WAS BESIDE himself. He had worked on the data all evening to make sure he had everything in place, then he reach for the phone.

"'lo," said a sleepy voice.

"Jake, wake up, man!" Milt shouted into the phone.

"Milt?" Jake asked sleepily. "What time is it?"

"Who knows? I've found the connection."

"Connection? What connection?" Jake was slowly coming awake.

"The connection between the four fires."

"I know you found the same accelerant and the same type of starters. We've been through this." Jake laid his head back on his pillow. His clock said the time was two a.m.

"Not that connection. The way the owners are all connected."

"The owners are not connected."

"Yes, Jake they are. I've been going through this data all day. I've found the link."

"What is it?"

"They all used the same security company."

"How does it connect them to the fires?"

"Jake, are you listening?" Milt was getting frustrated. "The security company is where Mark Stone was employed."

Jake sat up. He was wide awake now. "You Stone got access to the buildings from the owners when he was supposed to be providing them security?"

"Yep."

"Well, I'll be. Have you called Rachel?"

"Not yet," Milt didn't want to admit he didn't have a home number for Rachel.

"Let's wait until morning."

"Sure thing."

"And, Milt," Jake said, "thanks for calling me."

"No problem. I just wanted you to know I was carrying out my duties."

"Didn't occur to me you wouldn't."

"Night, Jake," Milt said softly.

"Night, Buddy," Jake replied.

The two hung up. Jake returned to his pillow and Milt went for another cup of coffee all the time thinking, *'he called me Buddy.'*

IT WAS NEARING midnight when Stone made his way to the Homestead. He carried three steaming cups of coffee and a bag with three sandwiches in it.

"Evening, Officers," he said as he approached them.

"Hello, what brings you out here?" asked one.

"Thought you could use a coffee and sandwich," said the elderly gentleman. "I've been watching you here for days."

"Thank you," said the other as he reached for a steaming cup of coffee.

"Do you usually have to stay this long at a fire scene?" he asked.

"No, but there was a murder connected to this one."

"Ah, I see," the old man nodded. "Bet you will be glad to be gone from here."

"Yeah, I'd rather be on patrol."

"Me, too. Give me a warm patrol car any day."

"Well, you boys enjoy the sandwiches."

"Thank you, sir," they said in unison.

The old man nodded and walked away. He knew they would be too busy to notice he was going down the alley. He would sneak in from the back. He wanted to know what was so interesting they were still on guard.

"Nice old guy."

"Yeah, too bad there aren't more people who appreciate what we do here."

"Well, when I finish this sandwich, I'll head around the building and make sure no vagrants have wandered in."

"Okay. I'll take the second round later."

The two men munched on the sandwiches and drank their coffee in silence.

Stone found his way into the basement and turned on his small flashlight. He gave the room the once over then said, "What have we here?" He had spotted the open door to the sub-basement. He quickly made his way down the stairs. He wondered what had been found here. It seemed to be untouched by the fire.

He walked to where the tunnels ended and found the other entrance. He left the same way and made his way back to his room.

His trip to the basement had been puzzling. It explained a lot about why there were still cops on patrol around the clock. Something interesting must have been down there. He wondered what it was.

He fell asleep and dreamed of the many things which could have been found in the sub-basement of the Homestead.

CHAPTER NINETEEN

Jake arose early the next morning. He had finished his breakfast and cleaned up when the phone rang.

"Good morning," Rachel said.

"What has you up so early?' he asked.

"Milt called, said he talked to you last night."

"More like early this morning."

"I've called Bos and we are meeting in Lt. Watson's office at nine. I thought you might want to be there."

"I'll be there. Hopefully with some lab information to add."

"I'll see you then."

Jake mused about how nice it was to hear her voice in the morning. But he did not waste time. He had some tests to run if he wanted to have anything to contribute at the meeting.

BOS HAD BEEN busy most of the night. He had been running down members of the illegal gun task force. He wanted to know what they had on Ike Howser. It had taken him hours to find out Howser was working with the FBI on a major score.

His conversation with Agent Todd was not the best.

"I don't have to tell you what Howser is working on," Todd said angrily.

"I know you don't, but we have a dead cop and confiscated weapons and Howser's name came up."

"Bos, Howser is one of the good guys. He was undercover for us."

"Why didn't his partner know?"

"Desmond had been undercover for two weeks when we learned about the gun shipment. Howser had no way to reach him. Howser reported running into Desmond near the Homestead."

"I take it neither man was able to talk to the other?"

"From what Howser reported, Desmond was acting like a derelict. He and Desmond made eye contact only."

"Does Howser know we have the weapons? Does he know Desmond is dead?"

"No to both. Howser is working with a Middle Eastern cell trying to find out where the guns are to go. He has no idea the guns have been confiscated. He did hear the Homestead burned, but since he did not know where Desmond was staying, he does not know Desmond is dead."

"We think the killer was another cop. Which might mean Howser's cover could be in jeopardy."

"I'll get word to him and we'll bring him in. He will want to help find Desmond's killer."

"Thanks. You know how to reach me." The big man held his hand out to Agent Todd. Todd took it and they shook.

As Bos was walking away, Todd said, "If it's any consolation, I know Desmond was one of the best."

"So do we."

THE MEETING WAS moved from Watson's office to a third floor conference room. Watson felt the conference room was larger and people would be more comfortable. He had also had the room swept for bugs. He was not taking any more chances and he was very interested in what they had learned. He was also angry because Stone had lost his tale the other night. Watson had wanted to know where he was when the time came to arrest him. He did not want to be in some big chase.

He had coffee and donuts on a back table. He had also added some fresh fruit. As people filed in they helped themselves and found a seat.

Bosworth was the last to arrive looking like he had been up all night.

"Sorry, Lieutenant," he said. "I had a hard time tracking down Ike Howser."

"Were you able to find him?"

"Sort of, but we'll come to it later."

"Since everyone seems to have arrived, we will begin," Watson said. "Who wants to go first?"

Rachel said, "I think we need to give the floor to Milt. He found the first lead."

Watson nodded to Milt. Milt stood and handed everyone a packet. He then began a power point presentation.

"The first three sheets in your packet represent the data collected at each of the four fires. You will see the same accelerant was used and there were two lines leading to the incendiary. The first line was a rapid burn. The second was slower and appeared to be a cigarette left in a book of matches. A burned book of matches and a cigarette butt were found at each scene."

"Meaning each fire was started by the same person correct?" asked Lt. Watson.

"Correct," Milt replied. "The next three sheets show each building owner met with two representatives from the Ridge Security Company. It also shows how soon after the meeting the fire was set."

"Do we think the owners are in on this?"

"We have not been determined yet. Someone will have to talk to each owner," Milt replied. "What we do know is Mark Stone worked for Ridge Security."

"Okay, what else do we have?"

Jake said, "I was able to get DNA from the first four fires on the cigarette butts they found. It all matches. DNA is being run on the butt found at the Homestead fire, it is expected to match. Once we have Stone in custody, we can get a DNA sample from him to see if the DNA we have is a match."

"Now are we to Ike Howser?"

"It seems Desmond saw Howser with the gun runners. He wondered if his partner had gone bad according to the notebook he kept," said Rachel.

"I spent all night running down Howser. He is working undercover with the FBI and an anti-terrorist task force. He was not aware of the fire or Desmond's death."

"Where does all it leave us?"

"Bos and I will take a photo of Stone with us and talk to Ridge Security and the owners of all the buildings which were burned," Rachel replied. "We need to know how Stone picked his buildings and why?"

Lt. Watson said, "We also need to know where Stone is. The tail I put on him the other night lost him. We have his picture at all the bus, train and airline terminals. They have been told to detain him and notify us. We figure something is keeping him in town."

They all nodded and then quietly left the room. Jake thanked Milt for his hard work. Then he headed for the fire department lab. He had reports to write. Rachel and Bos headed for the parking lot, they were going to Ridge Security.

CHAPTER TWENTY

The drive to Ridge Security took no time at all.

The manager, a Robert Swift, saw them right away.

"I don't want you to think Ridge Security had anything to do with the fires," Swift said.

"We want to know if you still have this man in your employ," Rachel said as she slid Stone's photo across the desk.

"No he left us last month. He said he had a job with a company in the south west some place," Swift replied. "Is he the man responsible for the fires?"

"We don't know yet. Did he leave a forwarding address?"

"I don't know, but I will have my secretary check," he said reaching for his phone. He buzzed his secretary and asked her to check with accounting and see if Mark Stone left a forwarding address.

While they waited he offered them some coffee. They declined. It was just a matter of minutes and the phone rang.

"Yes. I see, thank you." He hung up the phone and said, "Stone came in to pick up his last check three weeks ago. He left no forwarding address."

"I see do you have the address where he was living while he worked for you?"

"It should be in his personnel file." He walked to a file cabinet and pulled out a file. "Here it is." He took out a sheet of paper and handed it to Rachel. She copied the address into her notebook.

"Thank you, Sir," she said. "You have been most helpful." She rose and shook his hand. He offered his hand to Bos who also shook it, then the two left the office.

In the car she called Lt. Watson. "We have the address Stone gave when he was working for the security company. It was still good three weeks ago."

"I'll get a warrant and we'll send someone to check it out."

Rachel and Bos made their way to the office of Jasper Whitten. His was the first building burned. Mr. Whitten kept them waiting fifteen minutes while he got the company lawyer to his office. When they were all seated in his office he began, "I told the police everything I knew when the building burned."

"We are aware of your statement," Rachel replied. "Our investigation has turned up a possible suspect. We were wondering if you could identify this man." She handed him the photo of Mark Stone.

"I believe he was with the security company," Mr. Whitten said and handed the photo to his lawyer.

"Yes, that's right."

"Did you have any contact with him after the building burned?"

"Not any I can recall."

"Did anyone call you after the fire?"

"I'm sure someone from the security company did."

"Mr. Whitten, did you have any reason for wanting your building to burn?"

"What are you implying?" Whitten said indignantly.

"I'm not implying anything," Rachel replied calmly. "I have to ask questions in an investigation. Not all of them are pleasant."

"Right, right you are," stammered Whitten. "I had hoped to sell the building to some developers, but I had tenants with leases."

"What type of tenants?"

"There was a fruit market and a beauty shop on the lower floor and about four apartments still had tenants. I did not have them burned out."

"I didn't say you did. When would their leases have run out?"

"The apartments had four to six months on them and the two stores had at least six months a piece."

"What happened to the property after the building burned?"

"I sold it."

"And the tenants? What happened to them?"

"I helped each one of them relocate."

"Thank you for your help, Mr. Whitten," Rachel said as she stood to leave.

"Wait," Whitten said almost desperately.

"Yes."

"I got a call from a man after the building burned. He had a tape of me saying I'd be better off if it burned to the ground. He asked for money."

"Did you report this to the police?"

"No," he said sheepishly, "I just went ahead and paid him."

"How much did you pay?"

"Five hundred thousand dollars, in small bills."

"What! Why on earth did you pay him?"

"He had the tape. He said he would release it to the media. I would have been ruined."

"Tell me exactly how you paid this man. Did you meet with him?"

"No, I sent the money to a post office box."

"Do you have the address you sent it to?"

"Not any more."

"Did you get the tape from him?"

"No, I wish I had, he could still want more money."

"Thank you, Mr. Whitten; you really have been most helpful."

"Am I in trouble for this?"

"Not if you didn't hire him in the first place."

"I didn't, I honestly didn't," Whitten said frantically.

"Call tomorrow and you can come down and make a formal statement. You can bring your lawyer with you."

"I will," he said anxiously.

As Rachel and Bos left she said to him, "We need to have Lt. Watson talk to Billings. He might not have paid yet."

"We can only hope."

Rachel called the Lieutenant and reported what they had learned. She suggested he interview Billings while they followed up with the other two building owners. He agreed. Rachel and Bos headed for the next building owner.

STONE HAD DECIDED to take an early lunch. As he was eating in the diner near the park he saw several police cars heading toward his building. He watched for a few moments paid his bill and left.

Instead of going through the park and back to his building, he took an alley and headed east toward the docks. He knew of a place down there where he could hide.

He worried they might find his suitcase full of money, but it was only fifty thousand. The rest was safely out of the country. He was going to have to try to get into the building after dark and see what he could get. He did have the secret stash they would not find. It was enough to get him out of the country.

He had waited long enough. He was going to be out of town before first light. For now he just had to get to his hideaway and lay low for a few hours. Then he would slip away and be free.

AS RACHEL HAD feared the next two building owners had each gotten a phone call from someone with a tape recording of them saying they would be better off with their buildings burned. Like Whitten, they had both paid the unknown man. One had paid a million dollars and the other had paid one and a half million. The arsonist was getting more expensive by the building.

If Stone was the man, and it looked more and more like he was, then he had quite a tidy sum of money stashed somewhere.

Rachel called in and asked for a subpoena of all Stone's bank records. Then she realized she didn't know which bank he used. She asked to be transferred to payroll.

"Payroll, how may I help you?"

"This is Detective Adams. I need you to look up a former officer named Mark Stone. I need to know if he had a direct deposit of his pay checks and I need to know which bank they went to. I'm on my way in and will have all the proper documentation when I arrive."

"I'll check with my supervisor and see what we can do."

"Thank you."

Her next call was to Lt. Watson. She told him what she had done. He told her he would call Internal Affairs as they had done a thorough check on him just before he was discharged. She thanked him then turned to Bos. "You've been super all day today, Bos. You can drop me off at the station and call it a day."

"Thanks, I could use some sack time," he said. "You just call me when you are ready to bust this guy. I want to be in on this."

"You got it."

He let her out at the station and she went in to discover what she could about Mark Stone's banking habits. Bosworth headed to his apartment and bed.

CHAPTER TWENTY-ONE

J ake finished his reports and took them to Chief McDonald. He told the Chief he thought the case was about wrapped up and he would not be needed any more.

He went back to his lab and put all of the files together and filed them away. As he did something fell out of the file, he reached down to get it. It was Rachel's business card.

He was not looking forward to an evening alone. He knew he would not yet be able to go visit the Sullivans. So, without giving it much thought he picked up the phone and dialed Rachel's office. He got her voice mail and left a message to call him.

He decided to try her cell phone.

"Adams."

"It's Jake, would you like to get some dinner?"

"Sounds great! What do you say about eating in?"

"Your place or mine?"

"You come pick me up at the station and we'll figure it out."

"I'm on my way."

Rachel smiled as she snapped off her phone. Little did Jake know this was going to be a working dinner. She had all of the bank files on Stone. She started putting them back in the box they had come in.

Lt. Watson walked by. "Are you quitting already?"

"Nope, just moving to a different location."

He raised an eyebrow. "Oh, really?"

"Robins is coming by and we are going to get some dinner and go through this mess. Hopefully we can track Stone by his bank records."

"Good plan. Have a nice evening."

"Thanks, you too."

It was about five more minutes before Jake showed up. She pointed to the box and said, "We're going to need this."

"Hmmm. Must be this is going to be a working dinner."

"You got it right," she said smiling.

They left the building and Jake put the box in the back of his Jeep.

"So, Italian or Chinese?"

"Chinese sounds great! Do you know a good carry out?"

"Do I ever!" He started the car and they were off.

After a quick stop at Momma Sings, they went to Jake's apartment.

They had moo goo gui pan, Szechwan chicken, sweet and sour chicken, fried rice, egg rolls, crab rangoons, and, of course, fortune cookies. Jake had sweet and sour sauce in his refrigerator along with some hot mustard for the egg rolls. He made some tea and they sat down to dinner.

As Jake cleaned up after dinner, Rachel found some Amy Grant to put into the CD player. Then she sat down on the sofa with the box in front of her.

Jake found her there when he came in carrying coffee. "So, what are we digging into tonight?"

"The bank records of Mark Stone. We are trying to trace him through his banking habits."

"No leads on where he might be?"

"The cops found the flea bag he's been staying in. He was not there when they went in. They found a suitcase with twenty thousand dollars in it and a plane ticket for Brazil. They are staking it out. He's sure to come back."

"Did they leave everything there?"

"Yeah, they didn't want to scare him off."

"Well, then let's get started. How much are we looking for?"

"Somewhere around three million, seven hundred fifty thousand."

"You are kidding, right?"

"No, he got a half a million for the first building. The second was seven hundred fifty thousand."

"Let me guess, he got one and a half million for building number three."

"Yes, and two million for the last one, but he didn't get it the way he wanted."

"What made this one different?"

"The building owner, Jonathon Billings, III, thought he could catch Stone."

"What he did was make Stone wait around longer than he'd planned."

"So, we need to know where he has the money."

"Yep, it's our job."

"Let's get to it then."

She opened the box and handed Jake a stack of bank print outs. She took some for herself and they started working their way through them. At the bottom of her stack, Rachel found a report from Internal Affairs showing Stone to have more money than he could account for, but they could not figure out where it came from. He said he was moonlighting as a security guard, and they could not disprove it.

Jake got up to make more coffee and when he returned he found Rachel sleeping on the sofa. He found a blanket to cover her and turned out the lights. He took the stack of papers he had been working on and headed for his bedroom. He plowed through them making notes until midnight, then turned out the light and went to sleep.

ABOUT MIDNIGHT, STONE took the back alleys to his building. He went in through the basement window and climbed the stairs to his room. He entered without turning on a light. He made his way to the closet, found his suitcase and dumped everything on the bed. They had left the money, but he was sure they put a bug in the suitcase.

He took the pillow case off the pillow and filled it with the bills. Then he pried up the floorboard under the bed and took his fake ID and passport as well as the rest of the cash and put it in his pocket.

He quickly made his way back to the basement and out the window. He followed the alleys back to his waterfront hide away. Once there he turned on the flashlight he had stashed there weeks ago and assessed his chances for escape.

He thought his best bet would be to take one of the yachts moored in the harbor marina. He had been watching them for weeks. He knew which ones had been there for a while and which ones were new arrivals. He had his eye on one. He had even purchased gas so he would have some to put in the tank in case there was not enough to make his escape.

He had this as a back up plan just in case. All he had to do was get out onto the lake and motor to the St. Clair River. Then he would pull into one of the marinas and leave the yacht. He would book a flight out of Detroit or Toledo and be home free. The local cops would not have thought about the marina. It was not the logical place especially since he had left the ticket to Brazil in the room. He was not going to Brazil, but he was going to be a long way from here by sun up. He shut off the light, picked up his few things and made his way to the marina. He walked quickly to the yacht he had chosen and boarded it.

He stashed his few belongings, checked to see if there was enough gas to get him out of the harbor, and cast off.

He was unaware of the people on the next yacht watching his progress. He did not see one of them reach for a radio and make a call. He was sure he was untouchable.

CHAPTER TWENTY-TWO

J ake awoke to the smell of coffee and the sound of his shower running. It took him a minute to figure out why. Then he leaped from the bed flung on some sweatpants and headed for the kitchen. He poured a cup of coffee and started to make breakfast.

Rachel came into the kitchen with a towel wrapped around her head and wearing his bathrobe. She gasped.

He smiled thinking she looked cute dressed in his clothes and offered her a cup of coffee.

"I was going to make breakfast for you," she said.

"No problem. The smell of coffee was too enticing for me to stay in bed. I have a t-shirt and jeans you can borrow, check the bottom drawer in the chest."

"Thanks," she said as she walked to the bedroom. She came back a few minutes later wearing an old pair of jeans, and a blue t-shirt with a denim shirt over it.

"Looks good," he said as he dished up a breakfast of scrambled eggs, bacon, and toast.

"Mmm, this is delicious."

"Glad you like it."

"You're pretty handy in the kitchen."

"I like to eat so I learned to cook."

She laughed. "Well, it's one way to think of it. I like to cook, too."

"Good next time you make breakfast," he said smiling.

As Rachel cleaned up the dishes, Jake went to take a shower and get dressed.

"Rachel, I found something after you fell asleep."

"What?"

"Well, it seems our Mr. Stone has had money in several Ridge Cliff banks. Lately he has had them wire transfer all of his money to off shore accounts in the Cayman Islands."

"Great! We have an idea where he's headed." She grabbed her cell phone to call the Lieutenant. She did not get an answer.

"This is strange; the lieutenant isn't in his office. His secretary isn't answering either."

"Not so strange, it's Saturday."

She smacked her forehead, "Duh."

"It's been a busy week, so it's not hard to think you lost track of the days."

"Well I'll call his cell phone." She quickly dialed his cell phone.

"Watson."

"Lieutenant, this is Adams. Jake and I found something in Stone's banking records. He has put all his money in off shore accounts in the Cayman Islands. It's probably where he is headed."

"Makes sense; he stole a yacht last night and sped out onto the lake. He's probably heading for Detroit or Toledo. I'll alert the police in those cities and put out a BOLO. I'll also alert the coast guard as to where he might be headed. They are trying to track his movements right now."

"Ok, I guess all we can do for now is wait."

"Yes, enjoy the week-end. I'll call you if anything breaks."

She snapped off the phone and turned to Jake, "So, what have we got planned for today?"

He looked at her for a moment and then said, "How would you like to meet my family?"

"Sounds like an adventure."

They set off to Jake's parent's house. They had a sprawling ranch house on the west side of Ridge Cliff. Close enough to be considered in the Ridge Cliff mailing area, but far enough out to appear to be rural. It was a nice drive to the Jacobs' home.

Jake called ahead and told his mom to expect two more people for dinner. He was coming with a friend. On the way out he explained to Rachel his mom and step-dad lived at the ranch with two of his half sisters, Allison and Amy.

They spent a pleasant afternoon at the ranch. After dinner Jake offered to show Rachel around.

"I really like your family," she said as they walked toward the stables.

"Yeah, they're great," Jake agreed. All of the sudden he stopped.

"What's wrong?"

"Look," he said pointing to a small little house a short distance away.

"What is it?"

"It's the old stable hand's cabin." He turned and took Rachel by the shoulders, "Let's go get the keys, I have an idea." He grabbed her hand and they ran back toward the house.

Rachel was confused at his sudden change in direction.

"Mom," Jake yelled.

"What's all the fuss?" asked Mrs. Jacobs coming to the door.

"Where are the keys to the old cabin?"

"On top of the fridge, why?" she asked puzzled.

"I have an idea," he said excitedly.

She looked at Rachel who just shrugged her shoulders and shook her head.

Jake found the keys and grabbed Rachel's hand and headed back out the door.

"Jake, what on earth has gotten into you?" she asked.

"Don't you see we could fix it up?"

"Why would we want to? Are you thinking of moving back here?"

"Mr. Sullivan and Lupe."

Suddenly it dawned on Rachel what he was thinking. "It's a great idea!"

Jake opened the door to the little cabin. It really did not need much more than a good cleaning. The furniture was all there. By this time his family was coming into the cabin.

"Jake, is there something you want to tell us?" his mother asked.

"Yes," he said coming from the bedroom. "Have you thought of having anyone live here?"

"Are you planning to move back here?"

"No," he said and watched all the excitement fall from their faces. "What's wrong?" Then it dawned on him and he laughed. "No, I'm not moving back and neither is Rachel. I do have some friends in need of a home and this would be a great place for them."

"So, who are these friends?" his step-father asked.

"Mr. Sullivan and his granddaughter, Lupe. They were living at the Homestead when it burned. Mrs. Sullivan died from smoke inhalation. They've pretty much lost everything."

"How soon can they get here?" his mother asked.

"I don't know. How soon would you want them?"

"Give me a week to have this place aired out and everything thoroughly cleaned," she replied.

"I can."

"How old is Lupe?" asked Amy.

"She's six and a witness against the man who started the fire. She has a broken leg right now, but she'll be fine."

"Cool," his sisters said in unison.

Now it was settled Jake and Rachel headed back to Ridge Cliff. Jake dropped Rachel off at her apartment and told her to call if she needed anything. Then he went home. He called Rachel as soon as he got home.

"Adams."

"Rachel, do you think we can go to see the Sullivans tomorrow? I'd sure like to tell them we've found them a permanent home."

"I'd like to very much. Let's pick up some food and make it a day. They might be getting lonely."

"Okay, see you in the morning."

CHAPTER TWENTY-THREE

Jake and Rachel stopped to pick up some groceries before heading out to see the Sullivans. Both were excited about the news they had to share.

Lupe opened the front door and came running awkwardly to the car.

"Rachel, Jake, you're back!" she said excitedly.

"Sure we are, Sprite. Did you miss us?" Jake asked as he tousled her hair.

"You bet. Wait until Papa sees you."

Pat Sullivan opened the door as the three made their way in. Jake helped him put the groceries away. Pat made some coffee and they gathered around the kitchen table.

"What brings you out here?" he asked.

Rachel smiled and said, "Jake has some great news for you."

"I'm all ears."

"By this time next week, you will be in your new home," Jake said smiling.

"I've got no money for a home," Pat said seriously.

"You do for this one," Jake said. "It's small just two bedrooms, but there is access to a riding stable for Lupe."

"Jake, it sounds great, but I cannot afford it."

"Papa, please say yes, they have horses," Lupe begged.

"Pat, let me explain," Jake said, "it's on my parents' ranch outside of Ridge Cliff. It's the stable master's quarters. It's not much, but it's not being used. My sisters would love having someone around."

Mr. Sullivan's eyes teared. "How can I say no?"

"Great! Then it's settled," said Rachel. "Jake and I will be here on Saturday to get you and take you to your new home."

"How is the case coming?" Pat asked changing the subject.

"We are closing in on Lupe's bad man," Rachel answered.

"It looks like it will be all over but the trial in a day or two."

"What a relief. I didn't venture out much this week. I was afraid everyone might be someone looking for us. It will be nice to have a normal life again."

They had a pleasant lunch and Jake told Lupe all about his sisters Allison and Amy. She could hardly wait to meet them.

When they left to go home, Rachel pressed a couple of twenty dollar bills in Mr. Sullivan's hand. As she hugged him she whispered, "Buy a treat for you and Lupe."

Pat and Lupe stood in the yard waving until they were gone.

"See, Papa, I told you we'd be okay."

Pat looked down at his granddaughter and smiled, "Yes, my dear, you did."

They walked hand in hand into to cabin to do a thorough cleaning and talk about the new move they would be making. Pat knew it was going to be a long week.

MARK STONE HAD spent a week out on the water. He was looking forward to a shower, a good meal and a bed which didn't rock. He pulled into a slip in the yacht club in the Grosse Pointe Park area. He tied the boat up. Took all his belongings and headed to find a taxi.

He was surprised by two suited gentlemen who passed him then were suddenly at his side.

"Mark Stone?" one of them asked.

"Who wants to know?" he replied.

"Federal Marshals," said one. "You're under arrest."

Stone stumbled, but they caught him. One read him his rights while the other put him in handcuffs. They led him to a waiting car and transported him to the U.S. Marshal's office.

"Gentlemen," Stone said as he recovered, "I believe there's been a mistake. I'm a former police officer."

"Then there is no mistake," replied one of the Marshals.

Stone attempted to argue with the marshals, but when he found they would not respond gave up. He asked for a lawyer as soon as they allowed. One was appointed to him.

He stood mute at his arraignment his court appointed attorney speaking for him. He was transported back to Ridge Cliff to stand trial for the murder of Officer Miguel 'Mike' Desmond, the death of Mary Margaret Sullivan, and the arson fires in four buildings. There were related charges of extortion and blackmail.

Stone insisted there was a mistake. Offered no answers to questions by police and gave very little to his attorney. He could not believe this was happening to him.

Lupe bravely faced her 'bad man' and told the court what she had seen. Stone never took the stand in his defense and was sentenced to life without parole. The U.S. Marshall's office and Ridge Cliff police would spend years trying to trace all of the funds Stone had in accounts overseas. They confiscated those they were able to find. The first pay out of money were to the families of Officer Desmond and Mary Sullivan, then the police attempted to return some money to each person who had been blackmailed. Millions of dollars were still untraceable. Stone did nothing to help with the recovery of the money.

Ike Howser was able to bring in the leader of the Middle Eastern group who was scheduled to buy the gun shipment in the basement of the Homestead. The man was sentenced to prison. He also had a good lead on the supplier of those weapons. He was again undercover working on bringing the person to justice.

IT WAS EARLY in September, when they were finally able to bury Officer Desmond. He was given a full police honor guard. Word had been sent to his parents in Jamaica of his death. All the newspaper articles about him had been preserved in a scrapbook for them and tickets had been sent so they could attend the funeral. They had come and gone.

A few days later in a more private ceremony Mary Margaret Sullivan was laid to rest in a plot next to her son and daughter-in-law. Jake and his family, and Rachel attended as the priest said the words sending Mrs. Sullivan on to eternal life.

Pat and Lupe fit right in at the ranch. Pat had even put in a vegetable garden and kept them in fresh vegetables. Lupe was learning to ride and had started school again. Amy and Allison had taken her under their wing and were introducing her to all their friends.

Rachel and Jake had also been seen at the ranch a lot. Rachel too was learning to ride. Jake's mother enjoyed having them there.

Both were busy with their jobs and saw each other when time permitted. Their future was as yet undetermined, but Mrs. Jacobs thought she had an idea of how things might work out. She smiled as she put the finishing touches on the cake which would later help them celebrate Mr. Sullivan's birthday.

It was time to put the past behind them and start looking to the future. The Sullivan's future was here as a part of their family.

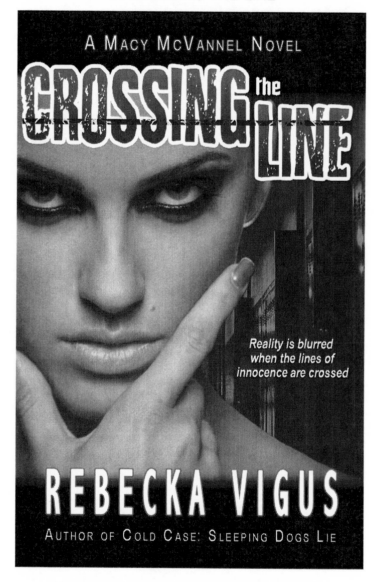

ACKNOWLEDGEMENTS

I would like to thank my editors once again for their fearless work at helping me put together my book. Donavee Vigus, who tells me I can't get her started and leave her hanging. Jamie Kline, who picks everything apart until I get it right. William Vigus, who gives me a man's perspective.

I also need to thank Brenda Butler for lending me her notes, books, and knowledge of arson and firefighting. I could not have done this without you.

Also, Diane Sather, who has helped me put together my marketing campaign, business cards, bookmarks and any other things I've needed done.

I know without them I could not have put all of this together and gotten it right. Thank you all.

Rebecka Vigus
August 2006

Special thanks to my wonderful cover and interior artists Blue Harvest Creative for all their hard work.
February 2014

ABOUT THE AUTHOR

Retired teacher Rebecka Vigus spends her time writing, reading, crocheting, hiking, and swimming. She travels seeking the ideal place to call home.

Out of the Flames is one of five mystery novels that she has written. The others include *Secrets, Target of Vengeance* and two Macy McVannel mysteries *Cold Case: Sleeping Dogs Lie* and *Crossing the Line*.

Ms. Vigus has been writing since she was in her pre-teens. Her first book was poetry, *Only a Start and Beyond*. She also wrote a self-help book for tweens and teens; *So You Think You Want to be a Mommy?*

Ms. Vigus has been listed as a Michigan Author and Illustrator at the state of Michigan website.

She loves spending time with family and friends. She is the mother of one and grandmother of four. She finds time to crochet preemie layettes for a neo-natal unit as well as hiking and swimming.

Find her at *www.ramblingsbyrebecka.blogspot.com*. All of her books are available at *amazon.com* and *barnesandnoble.com*

She is currently working on a new Macy McVannel mystery which will be available in late 2014.

CPSIA information can be obtained at www.ICGtesting.com
Printed in the USA
LVOW09s1435181114

414315LV00004BA/310/P